ANDREW BENSEN

# GENE AUTRY
## and the
## Golden Ladder Gang

An original story featuring
GENE AUTRY
famous motion picture star as the hero

*By*
W. H. HUTCHINSON

*Illustrated by*
ANDREW BENSEN

*Authorized Edition*

WHITMAN PUBLISHING COMPANY
RACINE, WISCONSIN

# CONTENTS

# ILLUSTRATIONS

*Gene Autry Nodded as He Looked at the Peaks*

# GENE AUTRY
## and the
## Golden Ladder Gang

## CHAPTER ONE

### THE GOLDEN LADDER

In the eerie half-light before sun-up of a desert morning, a lone rider broke his fireless camp and rode carefully out of a concealing tangle of mesquite and catclaw. He was a two days' ride east of the Colorado River, where the trail left the rim of the river valley and pitched upward along a ridge that ribbed down from the backbone of the Hualapai mountains.

The rider nodded to himself as he looked at the peaks above him. He had to be in the pass that led between them before the sun caught him under any hostile eyes that might be keeping lookout for strangers riding east. He lifted the bridle reins and squeezed the horse gently with his powerful knees.

The great chestnut sorrel took the trail with a tireless gait. He was a horse that warranted a second look any time or place. Even without the superb saddlery he wore, it took a second look to grasp his size and symmetry, so perfect were his proportions.

The man who rode him so easily and surely was built the same way. It was only after people looked at his eyes that they took notice of the compact, powerful body, and it was the eyes that betrayed the man's keen brain. They were laughing, dancing eyes with steel-gray flecks in them; the eyes of a man who would do "to ride the river with" and that was the highest praise in the West.

The man and his horse moved steadily up the trail and it was obvious that they shared a common bond of understanding and affection.

The rider's eyes didn't miss a single thing as they searched ahead and beside the trail. A heaped-up pile of rocks stood beside the trail with a stick thrust atop it. The rider spotted its significance in a momentary glance and when he spoke it was as much to the horse as to himself.

"That's an Indian post office, Champ," he said, and the horse turned his head as if to see for himself. "Yes, sir," the rider continued, "one Indian went by here two days ago and he left word he'd be back this way before the full moon. Pity that Johnny Hines couldn't be as thoughtful as that war whoop." His tone was wryly humorous and Champ nodded his head as if agreeing with his master. Gene Autry smiled at Champ's sensitive ears. "You're better company than most humans, Champ," he said. "You have brains enough not to talk before you think. That Johnny Hines now—" His voice trailed off into thoughts about the letter that had called him from his California ranch to make the long, long ride across the desert to answer the code of the West.

Johnny's letter had been a penciled scrawl on a crumpled sheet of paper:

*Dear Gene, Come a'runnin'. Johnny.*

It wasn't much of a letter but it was enough for Gene. Johnny needed him. Knowing Johnny's gift for trouble, his own or somebody else's, and knowing only too well that Johnny acted first and thought later, Gene had ample warning that whatever it was would be a man-sized assignment.

Gene was busy checking the distance to the pass against the onrush of the sun when a dull orange flower blossomed from a pile of boulders straight ahead of him up the ridge. The heavy bullet whined past his cheek like a spiteful wasp—*kuhzeeeen*—and Gene lifted Champ into a dead run right into the hollow, booming report of the shot.

Another flower of death bloomed amidst the pile of rocks but the dry-gulching shooter was wide with his aim. Gene had his rifle out of its boot under the *rosadero* and sprayed the rocks ahead with rapid fire. He didn't want to kill the unknown assassin, he wanted him alive for questioning, and his bullets chipped sharp splinters of rock around the hidden gunman's position with unnerving effect.

A blur of movement caught Gene's eye as Champ pounded up to the pile of rocks. The would-be killer was seeking safety in flight. Champ cleared the boulders in a mighty leap and raced to cut the running figure off from another darker blur that was his horse. Gene fired a warning shot and the fleeing bushwhacker changed direction and plunged down the side of the ridge into the depths of a steep canyon choked with scrub oak and mountain mahogany brush. The man's startled horse broke into a run and Gene laid Champ alongside him and snubbed the bridle reins to his saddle horn. They slowed to a gradual trot, and Gene wheeled Champ back onto the trail with the captured horse jogging docilely by his side. Whoever the unseen gunman was, he would have a long walk before he could report the failure of his mission. It had been too twisty a light for accurate identification of himself and Champ, and Gene's mind was left with only two alternatives. Either someone who didn't want him to meet Johnny *knew* he was coming, or, strangers of any kind were not welcome in Hualapai Valley.

Gene was still pondering the attempt to kill him when the trail topped out in the pass that overlooked the deep oval of Hualapai Valley to the east. The valley lay bathed in bright sunlight and as Gene turned in the saddle to look back down the trail, the sun climbed above the last rim of the mountains and threw the broken country into bold relief clear to the river. That bushwhacker would be hot and dry before he made water in either direction.

He dismounted in one flowing motion and ground-tethered the captured horse with the bridle reins. Carefully he loosened the cinch of Champ's saddle and aired his back to prevent galling. Then he cleaned the debris from the little spring that bubbled out of a granite outcrop in the pass and watched Champ slowly drink his fill. Gene unsaddled the captured horse and let him water and then drank himself.

The captured horse was a nondescript-looking animal compared to Champ. The saddle gear he wore was equally inconspicuous and work-scarred. Gene searched it unsuccessfully for marks of ownership or manufacture as he hung it, with the bridle and blankets, from a stub limb on a convenient piñon. He tied the horse to the same tree with the grass rope from its saddle and explored the brand on the horse's left hip with a practiced hand. His eyes narrowed to slits as he felt the scar welts from the branding irons. The original brand had been run-over into the present sprawling symbol that Gene knew went by different names in different sections of cattleland, Pigpen, Jailbars, Ladder, and was regarded suspiciously under any name.

Gene's thoughts were interrupted by a sudden movement of Champ's head. His ears pointed out their message and Gene quickly tightened the cinch and swung into the saddle. The clear bell-ring of a shod hoof on rock floated up the eastern side of the pass. Gene loosened his short gun in its hand-tooled leather holster and slipped his rifle from its boot into his lap.

Gene waited for the unknown rider, tensed and ready, until a vagrant gust of wind brought a fragment of unmelodious song to his ears. He relaxed, and a warm smile spread across his face. Only Johnny Hines could mangle a tune with such violence, and only Johnny Hines would let the world know that he was coming. The discord increased as the unseen rider neared the top of the pass and the words were clear on the thin mountain air:

> Ol' J. Johnny Hines was a man to admire;
> When he went to church he climbed up on the
>     spire;
> As he climbed to its top he looked way down
>     below;
> He said, "I'm goin' to Heaven the best way I
>     know."

Gene didn't wait to hear the next verse. He slid the rifle back under his leg, unhooked his riata from the tie-strap that held it, and swung to the ground. Running swiftly toward the eastern lip of the pass, Gene gained a little shelf of rock that overhung the trail just as Johnny rode carelessly beneath it. Swiftly Gene shook out a little loop, whirled it once and sent it snaking out to snatch Johnny's hat from his head. Johnny's reaction was typical of his nature.

He set his blaze-faced bay horse on its rump and whirled in the saddle, his freckled face wrinkled with anger and his fists clenched. Gene coiled in his line, with Johnny's hat bouncing fitfully at the end, looked blandly down at the man below him.

"I got your letter, Johnny," said Gene.

"Looks like you got my hat, too," said Johnny with a quick, warm smile flooding his face at the sight of Gene.

"Could have been your neck just as well," said Gene seriously. "Johnny, when in the name of tunket, are you goin' to start keeping your eyes open and your mouth shut?"

Johnny grinned sheepishly at this warranted reproof. "Aw, Gene," he said. "It was such a nice mornin' I just couldn't help singing and wanderin' up the trail."

"You'll keep doing that on nice mornings," snorted Gene, "and wake up to hear Saint Peter asking you how you want your harp tuned and what color strings you prefer. You ride on up to the pass and rest your saddle."

Johnny dismounted in the pass and aired out the bay's back before he watered him. Then he sat down against a boulder by the spring and explored his pockets for the makings. Gene took a seat beside him and waited until Johnny had a curly cigarette twisted into shape and duly lighted.

"Now, young fellow me lad," said Gene, "what's

gravelling your gizzard?"

"Hunh?" said Johnny. "Oh! You mean that letter
I wrote you?"

Gene nodded.

Johnny ran his hands through a mop of sandy red
hair that gave up a cloud of alkali dust, and frowned
to himself.

"Your brain work better when you irritate it?"
asked Gene quizzically.

Johnny grinned boyishly. "To tell you the truth
Gene," he said, "I was tryin' to figure out where to
start." His eyes fastened on the captured horse who
had swung around so the brand was visible to
Johnny.

"Where'd you get that horse?" he cried excitedly.

"Down the trail a piece," said Gene calmly. "You
know him?"

"Nunh-unh," grunted Johnny, "but he's wearin' a
Ladder brand and that's the big reason why I wrote
you that letter. What did he do, come nickerin' up
to you askin' for protection?"

"Not quite," said Gene with a grim twist to his
words. "Some jasper had him ground-hobbled while
he took a shot or two at a dim figure in the dawn's
early light. That was me. The jasper departed in
such a hurry he plumb forgot his horse. I didn't."

"They must be gettin' ready for somethin' special," said Johnny in angered tones. "They ain't
never started shootin' at strangers until they got into

*"Where Did You Get That Horse?" Asked Johnny*

the valley afore this."

"Johnny, you gabble like a guinea hen," said Gene in exasperation. "Just who is or are these people you call *they?* And what have you done now?"

"Me! What have I done?" asked Johnny in pained surprise. "For once in my life I didn't start nothin' but it ain't done me a smidgen of good. Trouble as usual, that's me." He paused in thought, then hurried on. "Yes, sir, when I done come over to the valley, I made up my mind to turn the other cheek like the Good Book says but when they stole my stove, while it was hot and my beans cookin' on it, I sent you that letter. They can't crowd Johnny Hines too far."

His aggrieved manner made Gene break out into laughter. "I got your letter," he said, "and I came ready, willing, and able to dance at your wedding, go your bail, or weep over your fresh-dug grave. Instead, I have to listen to you complaining that the world won't take you at your face value. I don't blame the world at all for that. Now you tell me who *they* is, or who *they* are!"

"Star Jordan," gritted Johnny, "Marshal of Hackberry, a star to his vest and a gun under his arm. Owns the Ladder brand, same's as on thet horse you collared, and the waddies that ride for him all look like they had stepped out of a poster that said: *Wanted for This and That, Mostly Felonious.*"

"Thought you knew better than to tangle with

the law," said Gene mildly.

"I do," said Johnny sullenly. "Only this time the law done tangled with me."

"Johnny," said Gene, "I can always tell when you've got a mad on."

"How?" asked Johnny quickly.

"Your mouth moves but your nose does the talking," said Gene, laughing. "Now you spell it out for me."

His laugh was so infectious that Johnny had to join in despite himself.

"Awright," said Johnny, "Here she comes. You see the valley down there?" His arm swung in a slow sweep from north to south.

Gene nodded. "That's Hualapai Valley, isn't it?" he said.

"Yep," said Johnny, "that's the Wollop-eye. Best cow country left in the Territory. Plenty grass, plenty water, not overcrowded it wasn't and no stock-killin' varmints. Lotsa little yellow bobcats that raise hob with chickens and suchlike but, shuckins, I didn't have no chickens. Yes, sir," he went on, "she was plumb ideal, but now she reminds me of a small-pox scar on the face of the earth."

Johnny's simile was pretty good. The valley reached forty miles from north to south. Hackberry Mesa jutted into it on the north, the broken *picachos* of the Sheep Skull Range hemmed it on the east, the squat mass of the Hualapais reared up on the west where the two friends sat and talked. Down the middle of the valley wandered the big Sandy, a river in rainy times, bone-dry ten months of the year, that plunged into a box canyon to seal the valley at the south.

"What's the matter with it now?" asked Gene. "Range war?"

"Nope," snapped Johnny. "Range hog. That self-same Star Jordan." Johnny was silent for a long minute, and Gene did not interrupt his train of thought.

"When you staked me to come over here and start my own outfit, Gene," Johnny said slowly, "I aimed to follow what I'd learned from siding you for the Association. I found me a good spring of water up in the north end of the valley, Spur Spring it's called. It was govermint land and I homesteaded it legal like a citizen has the privilege of doin'. I got me a couple of Hualapai bucks off the reservation that was willin' workers and we puttered around as happy as drunk ants. I built me a little 'dobe *casa,* built me some corrals and a water pen, laid in some beans, flour, sidemeat, and a couple of cases of airtights and spent the rest of our money, yours and mine, on a small herd of white-face cows."

"Didn't you plant no flowers to twine around the door?" asked Gene with a straight face.

"You go plumb to —" said Johnny and bit off the word. "Nosirreebobcat," he said, "I just can't ask you to go there. Hackberry's bad enough."

"Why?" asked Gene, "and where is it?"

"Jordan hangs out there, I done told you he was the marshal," said Johnny. "You see that mesa?" He pointed to the northern skyline.

Gene nodded.

"Right spang against the foot of that tabletop is Hackberry," said Johnny. "They's a canyon comes in from the east that the railroad used to get down off the high ground and cross the valley. Gerbode had him a store there, where a big spring of fine water come off the mesa. The railroad found it wouldn't rust the innards on their iron horses, so they made a dicker. Gerbode gets enough water for himself and his hotel, and the railroad gets enough for their engines and the section hands and whatnot they have stationed there. They was enough water left over for feed corrals and a big railroad stockyards for shipping cattle. Railroad built a turning wye there, waters their engines, hooks on and takes off helper engines, and otherwise lends an air of progress to the landscape."

"Johnny, I don't even have to go to Hackberry," said Gene.

"Why not?" asked Johnny, jumping in surprise.

"You've told me all there is to it," said Gene. "Why should I see for myself? You left out anything?"

"You're darn tootin'," said Johnny. "I was just tryin' to give you the proper background or whatever they call it."

"You've bent both my ears with that chatter of yours," said Gene. "Now you get down to the meat in the coconut."

"Jordan was usin' Spur Spring 'thout botherin' to take it up legal," said Johnny. "I homesteaded it and Jordan howled like a shot wolf. He tried to buy me off. I wouldn't sell. Then he tried to give me gentle little hints to move anyhow."

"Such as?" queried Gene.

"Shootin' my horses in the legs so's they was crippled but wasn't dead." Johnny's voice rose to a snarl at the remembrance. "Then I started sleepin' outside to catch them at it, and somebody dropped a dead skunk down my stovepipe and I couldn't use the house for a month. Then they stole my stove and I wrote you that letter."

"If Jordan can drive you off," said Gene, "before you've proved up on your homestead, it reverts to public domain and Jordan or anyone else can claim it. You figure that's what he's after?"

"*Seguro que si*," said Johnny. "Jordan done got the whole south end of the valley sewed up tight. If he can get Spur Spring in his grimy clutch, he's got the north end as well."

"Shuckins," said Gene, "if that's all that's bothering you, let's ride idly up to Mr. Jordan and make him see the light. I thought maybe you were in real trouble, like having a girl."

Johnny shook his head. "Gene, if it was only me and my troubles, I could take a lickin' and not whine none. But it's more than thet. Them riders of Jordan's they slap the Ladder brand on whatever comes their way, mostly other folks's cattle. If the owner pushes his complaint, he winds up in Jordan's jailhouse and by the time he gets through paying a lot of phony fines, he has to sell real cheap to get enough money to leave the country with his family." Johnny's voice registered his disgust. "And they's other things too!"

"Give them a name," said Gene.

"Well, another young fellow like me starts him a little place on govermint land, homesteaded legal, and his house burns up. Another rancher has a beef with Jordan and his house burns down. Mine's made of 'dobe and it won't burn either way. Then freight cars get robbed on Hackberry sidetrack. Ore wagons haul rich ore into town to ship to the smelter at Mayer and they just disappear, wagons, ore, and all. Herds of cattle disappear on their way to the railroad to get shipped and Jordan ships more cattle than he could possibly have."

"How about killings?" asked Gene.

"They ain't been none yet you could hang on the Ladder gang," said Johnny, "but they're workin' up to it as Jordan gets bigger and richer and more overbearin'. That's one thing I can't savvy," said Johnny puzzledly. "Jordan ain't the type to let a little blood stand in his way, but I reckon he'll get around to it."

"Looks to me as if you're really asking me to step into a whirly-go-round," said Gene.

"I am," said Johnny. "Why'd you think I sent for you? If it was just a case of whipping Jordan in a butting match, I could do it myself. But this thing is too deep for me. You got the brains and I—"

"You've got the temper," said Gene quickly. "Now you listen and I'll talk for a change."

"Suits me," said Johnny, leaning back against the boulder behind him. "You can sing me a song if you want to real bad."

"I'll sing you a song you won't like," said Gene affectionately, "but not right now. You tell me why the decent folks in Hackberry and the valley don't put a spoke in Mr. Marshal Jordan's wheel?"

Johnny seemed taken by surprise. "Why, Gene," he said, "I don't rightly know. For one thing, they ain't many of them and for another thing," he looked at Champ, "my shining silver-mounted friend, they lack leadership."

"How many real good men and true can you count in Hackberry?" asked Gene, trying to pin Johnny down to facts.

"I don't have to shed my boots to do it," said Johnny. "The railroad people, they don't count 'cause they keep to themselves and they don't have nothin' worth stealin'. Prospectors, drifters, Indians, and the like, they ain't a stable element. That leaves

Gerbode who owns the store and Pres Wesley, the freighter, and me and you for a total of four. Mebbe we can count on 'Relio Baca and his kinfolks, and I don't know how many that'd make."

"Baca's Spanish?" asked Gene.

"Real dyed-in-the-saddle-blanket," said Johnny. " 'Relio owns the last Spanish grant in the Territory, it lies over the other side of the Sheep Skulls mostly, and 'Relio bosses it just like his granddaddy did when the Bacas was the biggest thing between here and *Ciudad Mexico*. Funny thing about 'Relio," said Johnny, "he's got hair that's redder than mine and skin just as white—"

"And a sight cleaner," said Gene quickly.

"His eyes are so blue that they fool you," said Johnny unperturbed. "They look like china. But Baca and his *gente,* they keep strictly to themselves."

"You figure to blame them after what you've told me about the caliber of these so-called citizens that's clutterin' up this neck of the woods?" asked Gene.

Johnny admitted the truth of this remark by shaking his head.

"I don't either," snapped Gene. "You all through countin' the forces of law and order around Hackberry?"

"That's all they is," said Johnny. "Just the four of us, not countin' on Baca and not includin' J. Francis Gosslen either way."

"Why not and who is he?" said Gene.

"Well," came Johnny's drawl, "this Gosslen gent has a law shingle hung out, he lends money to the people that play in tough luck and he's a quick gent with a foreclosure. He dresses like a gambler and talks like a parson." Johnny's voice curled in contempt for a man who made his living in such fashion.

"Where'd he come from?" asked Gene, a faint recollection stirring in the back of his mind.

"Oh, he got off an eastbound train in Hackberry some months back," said Johnny. "Give it out that he'd left California for his health."

"He did," snapped Gene, and Johnny's jaw dropped.

"If it's the same gent," said Gene, "and your description tallies, he worked for Wells Fargo until they caught up with him."

"What was he doin'?" gawped Johnny.

"He had his own system of dividin' the cash," said Gene. "He threw it up in the air and what stuck to the ceiling went to the company." Gene's fine eyes showed his opinion of a man who would betray his trust.

"I'll be darned," said Johnny. "He talks smooth and oily but I never figured he'd dare steal from a rabbit. He runs more to doing it in the odor of legal sanctity."

"You been reading books again?" said Gene mildly.

"Only the saddle catalogue," said Johnny.

"Why do you ask?"

"You got some new words rolling off your tongue," said Gene. "Maybe you been courtin' a school-ma'am."

Johnny shook his head. "None of 'em single in these parts long enough for me to more than look at 'em," he said. "Then they marries somebody else with a steady job."

Gene grinned at the frank disappointment in Johnny's voice. "Well, let's get riding," said Gene, springing to his feet.

"What's your plan?" asked Johnny.

"We turn this Ladder horse loose and let him join the wild bunch or go home, whichever he wants," said Gene, "then you and I mosey into Hackberry by separate ways and dig around until we find what we want."

"What's that?" said Johnny. "Shuckins, it won't be hard to find Jordan. You can smell him."

"We'll find Jordan when we want him," said Gene, "but what we want first of all is to find who is the real top to the Ladder, the golden ladder that Jordan has propped against Hackberry to pick it clean."

"You think too fast for me," confessed Johnny. "I'd settle for Jordan and clean him up. But then, I never did win any medals for looking way down beneath the surface. You tell me what and when, and I'll do it."

Gene nodded. "Just like always, Johnny," he said. "Now, when we meet in Hackberry, we don't know one another and we might even be real unfriendly. If I rode into town siding you, Jordan would tag me with your label—Ladder hater."

Johnny nodded his head in agreement.

Gene never changed his expression nor his tone of crisp, confident command. "And another thing," he said, "think how I'd feel coming into a new community with no better recommend than an outfit like yours riding alongside of me."

Johnny started to nod his head, and then snorted as Gene's remark hit home. He let his eyes rove over the magnificent saddle and trappings that Champ wore so proudly. "Anyone aimin' to dry-gulch you can't complain that they ain't got a target," said Johnny dryly. "That feller this mornin' must have been blinded by the sight.

"Gene," said Johnny seriously, "I mean it. That outfit of yours is sure goin' to make you stand out like a brass rail in a saloon. In this country, that ain't healthy."

"Johnny," said Gene patiently, "I like fine saddle gear for a champion horse. If Hackberry wants to think I'm nothin' but a four-flushing dude on a showy horse, that's all to the good. Maybe we can surprise 'em if they'll just think that way long enough."

"You always do take the biggest risks," said Johnny. "You still got your Association credentials?"

"You bet," said Gene. "Stockmen's Association papers and since I didn't know what kind of a jackpot you were in, I sent telegrams to Burton Mossman in Phoenix and one to the big head of the railroad. I am a Special Territorial Ranger and a Special Railroad Agent. All those lawful powers make me round-shouldered from carrying them."

"That's just fine, Gene," said Johnny. "You do the thinkin' and I'll do the strong-man act. How's that?"

"You always did take the easy part," said Gene, laughing. "Let's ride."

Johnny left the pass first, swinging up and out along the spine of the mountains to enter Hackberry from the north, his usual direction when entering town.

Gene watered Champ before he swung into the saddle and paused to look out across the valley below. His eyes fixed the lay of the land in his mind, and they noticed something Johnny had forgotten. A windmill flashed its arms in the sun between the foot of the trail and Hackberry. "That's all to the good, Champ," said Gene affectionately, " 'cause she'd be a dry crossing otherwise." Champ tossed his head and rolled the bit wheel under his tongue as if in answer.

They were halfway down the rocky trail to the valley when Gene spotted a dust cloud rising slowly above the valley floor to his right and far below. An unforeseen element was entering Hualapai Valley to cloud the search of Gene Autry for the top of the Golden Ladder gang—and to play havoc with Johnny Hines in the process.

# CHAPTER TWO

## COOL WATER COMES HIGH

To an untrained eye or a hasty mind, the cloud might have been a dust devil dancing across the valley floor, or the alkali column stirred up by a band of wild horses. But to Gene Autry, skilled in interpreting the signs of nature and of man, the dust was raised by a bunch of cattle, a small herd probably not over a hundred head.

Two riders escorted the cattle, one on either side, and a little band of horses and pack mules stirred up their own mark of passage behind the trail herd and a little to one side. Gene filed this knowledge in his mind and made his plans to intercept the trail herd before they reached the windmill he had spotted. With only two riders to handle them, the cattle would be hard to control once they smelled the water that the windmill promised. By the code of the West, it was only common courtesy to lend a hand when needed.

Gene turned his thoughts to the problem of Hackberry and the Ladder gang as Champ picked his sure-footed way down the trail. Even without Johnny Hines's suspicions and the threats he had experienced, the very fact that Jordan was running the Ladder brand warned Gene to be on the lookout for skulduggery. No honest man ever ran a Ladder brand. The reason was simple and obvious. The very shape and make-up of the Ladder, two vertical marks connected by four horizontal bars, lent itself to covering, not a multitude of sins, but a multitude of other brands. A Ladder brand was a sure source of extra cattle to men schooled in the tricky artistry of a running iron. The fact that Jordan, by Johnny's testimony, was waxing richer and more powerful with each passing season, added strength to Gene's belief that the Ladder brand was one good reason for suspecting the honesty of Star Jordan's income. Also, when a man ran the Ladder brand and hired a crew of gunslicks, the two factors confirmed one another—crooked brand and a crew to use it.

Gene knew and understood these two factors from his long work with the Stockmen's Association. They could be handled and brought to book. But, if there was a different type of mind behind these obvious realities, why then the case called for real savvy. It wouldn't do the decent people of Hackberry much good to scotch the snake unless they got its head at the same time.

Gene was engrossed in his thoughts as he rode down onto the uneven floor of the valley itself. Champ had been guided by the instinctive pressure of Gene's powerful knees, and they intercepted the little trail herd at the point Gene had selected. The tormented bawling of thirsty cattle brought him out of his study and his keen eyes grasped the situation at a glance.

The lead cattle had smelled the water at the windmill although it was still hidden from them by a slight swell in the valley floor. They were stringing out to reach it, the ambling gait of driven cattle increasing in tempo to a shuffling trot that Gene knew would break into a headlong stampede that spelled disaster. Cattle that rushed to water with the heat of their travel still on them, drank too much too quickly and might die. No cowman worth his salt could see this happen no matter whose cattle were involved. The riders he had spotted from above were not in position to check the rush, and Gene acted swiftly to save the day.

He lifted the bridle reins and spoke softly to Champ. The great horse galvanized into a deceptive lope toward the point of the herd. Champ's gait was deceptive for two reasons. His rider seemed to flow with him over the ground and the horse himself gave no sign of straining effort, yet if you could have measured his tracks, they were far apart and spanned a lot of ground between each set of hoofprints.

The feel of the horse between his knees, the pounding wind against his face, brought the blood racing through Gene's veins and his whole body responded to the thrill of the race. The lead cattle were plunging in full flight for the windmill water and as Gene raced along the panting, bawling mob, he noticed that they were all steers—big steers, thin and weak and gaunted from thirst, and now made crazy by the promise of relief.

They reached the point of the herd where a big brindle steer with foam-flecked muzzle led the stampede. His long sharp horns flickered wickedly in the dust as he swung his head from side to side as he ran. Gene kneed Champ ever so gently and the great horse responded with an extra burst of speed that brought him alongside the racing animal. Gene's hat came off in a sweeping arc and he beat the brindle steer in the face with it, leaning boldly from his saddle right into the arc of the pointed horns. Steadily and surely, Gene and Champ deflected the lead steer from his headlong rush. The balance of the herd followed their leader into the beginnings of a big circle that slowly turned in upon itself, like a cat chasing its tail, until they milled in a tight and compact knot. Gene's superb cow-sense, daring riding and quick thinking had saved the steers from self-destruction. There was no thought of this nor of self-praise in Gene's mind as he drew out to one side while the steers milled in bawling perplexity at the sudden turn of events.

There had been no sign of the two riders with the herd during Gene's singlehanded success at turning the stampede. This was no sign that they were lacking in gumption or in good sense. "They may have had troubles of their own, Champ," said Gene, and began to beat the thick layer of dust off his clothing.

The two riders would show up when they got around to it, and in the meantime, the steers were safe and that was all that interested Gene. A friendly whinny from Champ, a whinny that seemed to say, "Here we are and we did a good job too," signaled the approach of two riders from the direction of the milling herd. It was hard to make them out through the pall of dust that rose above them, but at about the same time Gene spotted them, they spotted him and the two figures separated, to come at him one on either side.

This wasn't the way Gene had expected it. It looked suspicious. Two riders splitting up to approach a single rider spelled a desire to hook him in a cross-fire and Gene smiled a little thinly to himself and waited. If they wanted fight, they'd get fight. If they wanted friendship, that was what they would get. It was up to them, not Gene.

The rider on his right drew Gene's attention first because he came up the quickest, his spurs drumming a slow tattoo on his horse's flanks. He was short and grizzled, with a square stubby beard hiding his face. The mark of a long trail was on his horse and on his worn denim brush jumper and in the dusty creases of his floppy black hat. He wore the bullhide bat-wings of a Texas cowboy and his double cinched hull with the squatty horn for a tied rope confirmed his origin.

Gene took in these details and another salient fact came home to him with the click of a cocking hammer. The rider held a short-barreled carbine across his waist, hidden below the saddle fork, and the muzzle centered on Gene's stomach.

The other rider had taken advantage of Gene's predicament to spur up on his left. Gene was careful not to turn his head nor to take his gaze off the rifle rider to his right, but from the tail of his eye, he noticed that the second half of the pincers movement at least had no artillery in firing position. The first move would come from his right and Gene evolved a plan of action to meet it when the time came.

He gazed levelly at the man with the rifle and this worthy gazed steadily back without changing the position of the menacing rifle in the slightest, while his jaws moved rhythmically over an egg-sized lump in the side of his jaw. The silence was complete except for the bawling of the milling steers and Gene began to put his plan into action.

The unnoticeable pressure of his knees against Champ's sides was answered by a slow gathering and bunching of mighty muscles that was not revealed by any outward ripple. Gene felt the gathering tension in the horse beneath him, like the tightening of a coiled steel spring, and grinned to himself. When

*The Muzzle Centered on Gene*

he gave the signal with his knees, Champ would explode in an incredible burst of movement that would carry them past the rifle muzzle before even a cocked trigger could be pulled. Chances were it would be pulled, only to miss, and then before a fresh cartridge could be levered into the breech, Champ would pivot on his hind legs and Gene's gun would hold the balance of power, if there was any further argument. Of course it was risky, but it was a considered risk and Gene always remembered his mother's saying: "You can't fry eggs without breaking them."

The slow building up of power to be suddenly released was almost finished, then it was finished and Champ was poised and ready, the pulsing flow of power beating up at Gene from every fiber of his horse. Gene screwed himself down in the saddle and his knees began their quick signal of contraction when a voice brought all his plans to naught.

It was a rich pleasant voice, that was made for throaty laughter that would stir the senses, but now it was filled with anger. "What right have you to interfere with my cattle?" said the voice and Gene could not believe his ears. It was the voice of the rider on his left and the voice was that of a young woman.

Gene thanked his lucky stars that she had spoken when she did, even in anger. If he had given Champ the signal, she might have been hurt in the fracas that would have followed, and it was not in Autry's scheme of things to hurt a woman at any time.

Gene did not answer the imperious question until he felt Champ relax beneath him. Then he kept his eyes fixed on the short rider with the rifle as he said, "I'm going to tip my hat to the lady just so's you won't think I'm unmannerly."

There was more to it than just his words. If he had made a sudden move, without explaining it, it might have been misinterpreted by the rifle.

The rifle never wavered a hair's breadth from the pit of Gene's stomach as the short man chewed his cud a silent moment and let a stream of tobacco juice slide out one corner of his mouth to deluge an unwary lizard. Satisfied with his aim he nodded his head in time with his words. "You go right ahead," he said. "Tip yore hat to Miss Hardesty and speak yore piece. She done asked you a question."

Miss Hardesty had spent the time appraising the horse and the rider who had saved her cattle, and she evidently didn't like what she saw. Before Gene could remove his hat, her voice cracked out at him, although it was addressed to the third party present.

"Give him time, Boomer," she said. "He's probably thinking about how pretty he looks and can't be bothered about interfering with other people's property." There was more than a sneer in her tone; there was anger that was close to tears.

*I hope she doesn't cry* was Gene's thought as he

removed his hat in a gesture worthy of a plumed cavalier, and turned slowly in the saddle to face the girl. It was hard to tell what lay beneath the powder of alkali dust that overlaid the girl and her riding clothes and the horse beneath her, but not even the dust could conceal the anger in her snapping brown eyes nor the worried frown that accented the strong character of her oval face. Gene had barely time for this first quick survey before her voice was hammering at him again.

"I asked you a question. By what right do you interfere with my cattle?" she said, and her tapping quirt beat against her divided riding skirt of fringed buckskin in time with her words.

Gene had a hard time keeping curtness from his own voice but the worry that lay beneath her words like a living sore, let him excuse her rudeness.

"Why, Miss Hardesty," he said, "has someone been hindering your lawful property?" The calculated civility of his question seemed to stir the girl to greater anger.

"Yes!" said the girl named Hardesty, "you have caused me to lose precious time on the trail besides which, the way you choused those steers ran off dollars in good weight. Of course," she went on, "I suppose it's asking too much of a dressed up dude to understand that weight on cattle and time on the trail mean money to working cowmen."

"I suppose you are asking a lot, Miss Hardesty,"

was Gene's reply, and its double meaning apparently went unnoticed by the worried girl. "Now, let me ask you one simple question," said Gene. "How long since your steers were watered?"

The girl seemed startled at Gene's directness but she answered quickly, as though water was a thing she kept uppermost in her mind. "We watered yesterday morning," she said, "on the other side below False Divide." Her arm swung toward the south end of the valley where the Sheep Skull Range ran down to meet the box canyon of the Big Sandy. "We've had no water since then and it's still a long way to Hackberry and the railroad corrals."

Gene nodded his head in agreement while his mind immediately registered the knowledge that she was a stranger to the valley if she had come in over the broken ridges of the Sheep Skulls. Then, too, she was headed for the railroad corrals at Hackberry, which fact, coupled with anxiety over her steers losing weight spelled out that she intended to sell her little herd at the railroad. She had reason to be concerned with unnecessary chousing of her cattle but even this did not excuse rudeness.

Gene was so busy fitting these new pieces into the puzzle of Hualapai Valley, that he did not notice the intent gaze the girl had fixed upon him. Even if he had, it is doubtful that he would have guessed the thoughts that went running through her mind. *He certainly is good looking and what I wouldn't give to own that magnificent horse.*

When Gene looked up at her, she lowered her eyes suddenly and then raised her head as if waiting for him to explain himself. Little devils of impish fun danced in Gene's eyes as he figured out how he could make this spitfire trap herself and thus get him an unspoken apology for her actions.

"I guess your steers are pretty dry by now, Miss Hardesty," he said, and his voice played up her opinion of him as a prettied up dude.

"Of course they are dry!" Disgust was in her tone and in the shrug of her shoulders. "And they won't be any easier for the two of us to handle now that you've stirred them up playing cowboy."

Gene grinned and let her taunt go unanswered. "Well, then," he said, "seeing as how I did all this damage, I just naturally will have to help you get them to the next water."

Micaela Hardesty, for that was her full name, snorted, if any woman of her charm could snort, and called across Gene's shoulders to the watchful rider behind him. "You better catch us fresh horses, Boomer. The gentleman here wants to help us drive to Hackberry." She paused as if choosing her words, then said, "And that means we really will have our work cut out for us."

Gene waited until she had finished and then raised his voice to be sure that Boomer could hear him too. "I think you misunderstood me, Miss," he said as the

girl looked at him almost scornfully. "I said I would
help you to the next water, not to Hackberry."

Micaela Hardesty's face reflected her surprise.
Gene's voice hardened a little and if Johnny Hines
had been there, he would have recognized its tone.

"Miss Hardesty," said Gene, "there is a windmill
over that little rise in the ground up ahead. I stopped
your cattle to keep them from foundering themselves and dying where they stood in the water pen.
I can assure you," he continued, "that it is no pleasure for me to run cattle at any time and particularly
cattle that belong to people who can't control them!"
His last sentence cracked like a rifle shot, and he
was ashamed of himself when he saw it take effect
on the girl before him.

Her face dissolved into tears and her slender,
rounded shoulders shook convulsively as she fought
to keep from sobbing out loud. Gene made an instinctive movement toward her, with a sincere desire
to correct his churlish attitude, when a dry and
deadly voice behind him checked him short.

"You've done made her cry, you four-flushing
dude. Now git. Or I'll blow you in two shore's my
name's Boomer Banning."

Gene wanted to wheel Champ in his tracks and
ride the man down, this kind of talk he understood,
when Micaela Hardesty's voice again intervened.

"Boomer, you stop that! Do you hear?" Her voice
was again the voice accustomed to obedience, and it

brought a disciplined response from her henchman.

"Yes'm, Miss Micky," said the grizzled Banning, "I'll let him go—this time."

"Boomer," said his boss lady, "we aren't going to let Mr. — Mr. —"

"Autry, Miss Hardesty, Gene Autry," said Gene politely.

"That's a nice name," said Miss Hardesty, "it's another reason why we aren't going to let you go without thanking you for doing what you did. And," she smiled appealingly at Gene, "without apologizing for my rudeness. You will help us to the windmill, won't you, Mr. Autry?"

Gene could not help but nod his smiling desire to help her drive to the windmill. Whenever a person met him halfway, Gene was sure to go the other half, and more. This Hardesty girl had what it took; she could make a mistake and then confess it without hiding behind the fact that she was a woman. Gene felt himself attracted toward her forthright personality and during the drive to the windmill, he had plenty of time to find other attractive features in Micaela Hardesty.

They lined out the steers in trail herd style for the windmill, the big brindle brute again taking his rightful place in the lead. Gene took the hardest position, riding in front to check the herd and keep them from again stampeding in desperate thirst for the water that their acute nostrils could scent from afar. Micaela and the grizzled Banning rode slowly up and down either side, from point to swing and back to drag until the bunched-up steers were strung out in orderly procession. Then Micaela rode a wide circle around the procession, to join Gene Autry in the lead, with the wish in her heart that she had a mirror and some other fixings with her.

As she rode slowly up to him, she was surprised to hear a song welling up in a fine and powerful voice from the man atop the chestnut sorrel stallion. It was a joyous tune and the singer's voice belied the almost tragic meanings of the words he sang.

> *All day I face this barren waste*
> *Without the taste*
> *Of water.*
> *Cooool water. . . .*

Micaela's mind raced madly for the proper approach and then she found it. She rode up to Gene, smiled shyly at him and extended the burlap-wrapped canteen that dangled from her saddle. "It isn't cool, Mr. Autry," she said, "but it is wet."

"Thanks, Miss Hardesty," said Gene, "but we'll be there soon, there's the windmill arms just ahead. Besides," Gene grinned in his turn, "I have a mouthful of wet." He put his hand to his mouth and spat a small round pebble into it. "It's an old 'Pache trick to keep your mouth from drying out. Doesn't do you much good but it does keep you from thinking about how thirsty you can get."

Micky Hardesty looked at him with ill-concealed amazement. The more she saw of this stranger, the more she realized that there was something to him that didn't meet the eye on first glance. She was more than ever conscious of her dusty, trail-worn appearance and tried to make up for it with conversation.

Gene learned a lot about Micaela Hardesty in the next half-hour, and what he learned only increased his respect for the girl and deepened his understanding of her temperamental outburst when they first met. This little bunch of drouthed-out steers was practically all that was left of the once powerful Boxed H outfit that had been her father's pride and joy. Big Mike Hardesty had come out of Texas behind his longhorn cattle, with his new wife and one pack mule for their few belongings. He had settled in the broken angry country along the Rio Burro, southeast of the Sheep Skulls, and had carved out a cattle kingdom for himself as big as some states back east.

In spite of high water, heat, rustlers, or bronco Apaches, Big Mike had endured and grown great. Then his wife had died before her time, and the joy of living had died with her. Big Mike had let the Boxed H run down and then he too had headed, almost gladly, said the girl, down that lonesome trail where all the pony tracks point just one way.

The Boxed H riders had jingled off into the sun-

set looking for other jobs where the pay was certain
and only Boomer Banning, who had followed Big
Mike out of Texas, was left to help Micaela bring
this pitiful remnant of a once great outfit to the railroad. When she sold them, Micaela confided to
Gene, she was going to split the money with Banning
and then she was going to California to find a job in
the city.

Only one question puzzled Gene as he listened to
this outpouring and he finally put it into words.
"Why are you so certain that you can sell these steers
in Hackberry, Miss Hardesty?"

The girl looked up at him in astonishment. "You
can always sell steers in Hackberry, Mr. Autry,"
she said. "Mr. Jordan always has a buyer and besides,
he sent me a message that whenever I got there, he
would dispose of my cattle for me."

Gene digested this startling information in silence
while his mind saw the simplicity of altering a Boxed
H brand into a Ladder. Yes indeedy, Star Jordan was
running things with a high hand when he felt sure
enough to ask a girl to drive her own cattle right into
his stronghold.

One look at the face of the girl as she told him of
her past, and her hopes for the future was enough
to make Gene hold his tongue about Star Jordan.
He knew enough about Micaela Hardesty already to
put him in mind of the old horse breaker's saying:
"You don't have to know more than the horse; you

just got to have more time." And the time to talk cold turkey to the Boxed H boss was not now because the windmill water pen was right before them and the bars were up between the cedar gate posts.

Gene touched Champ with his knees and Micaela hit her horse a token lick with her quirt. They raced ahead of the lead steers to get the bars down before the frantic cattle piled up against them with crippling effect.

Gene hit the ground in a running jump as Champ plowed four feet into a braking stop. He had the top bar down and thrown aside and was wrestling the middle one out of the gate slots, when a scream from Micaela made him jump, wheeling in mid-air with his hand darting for the gun at his hip.

He was too late! A double-barreled shotgun at full cock looked him square in the middle.

The man who held the shotgun had materialized from the protecting pickets that enclosed the bottom of the windmill outside the water pen. He acted as if he knew how to pull the triggers on the sawed-off Greener in his hands. A high-cheekboned face gave a hint of Indian blood and his eyes were glittering dots of black obsidian. His voice confirmed his ancestry.

"You pay first," he grunted, "or you no water cattle."

Gene was dumfounded. It was an unwritten law in the cow country that one stockman did not charge another for water for his cows, or himself.

Gene thought fast. He looked at the man behind the shotgun and he didn't look like the type who'd build a windmill for himself. "You own this windmill?" asked Gene.

The man looked at him coldly. "No own um," he grunted again, "me win'mill wrangler, watch-up, fixum."

"Who does own it, then?" persisted Gene.

"Him belong Star Jordan," was the disdainful answer.

Micaela's voice cut in to the conversation. "Mr. Jordan is selling my steers for me," she almost sputtered. "I know he wouldn't charge me for watering them."

The windmill wrangler looked at her impassively. "You water win'mill, you pay," was his verdict.

Miss Hardesty was going to have apoplexy—at least that's the way she looked—and what she said to the windmill wrangler would have peeled the shell off an armadillo. Not the words, but the way she said them. The Indian never batted an eye but his attention was riveted on Micaela's face which gave Gene the opportunity of signaling Champ with his hand.

The horse eased himself forward, pace by pace, with his head outstretched and lowered until Gene signaled him to stop. The windmill wrangler took no notice of this action and Gene heaved an inward sigh of relief. Micaela's voice was frantic now; her

steers were crowding closer and closer and still the
stubborn windmill wrangler refused to heed her
pleas.

"But I tell you, I haven't enough money to pay
the ridiculous charges you say Mr. Jordan demands
you collect," she cried.

Once again Gene detected the approach of feminine tears in the Hardesty voice. It was time for him
to put his plan in action.

"Don't argue any longer, Miss Hardesty," said
Gene, apparently not looking at the Indian or the
shotgun. "I'm going to take down these bars and we
can talk about paying for water later."

He half turned as if to carry out his threat and
the Indian grunted a matter-of-fact warning. "No
pay, you touch bars, me pull trigger."

"Champ!" cried Gene, and the horse threw his
great head high into the air with a whistling snort.
The windmill wrangler was taken by surprise. His
eyes instinctively followed Champ's head for a split
second and that was enough.

Gene's right arm flashed down and up. There was
one barking report from his gun and the shotgun
was torn out of the Indian's hands by the crashing
impact of a well-aimed bullet, to explode harmlessly
in mid-air as the set triggers failed to hold under the
shock. Before the wrangler knew what was happen-
ing, Gene had him by the throat, and his blazing
eyes spoke just as loudly as did the muzzle of his

*Gene Grabbed the Wrangler*

gun that jammed the Indian's stomach.

"Now you listen to me," said Gene. "You were just following your orders from Jordan. I don't hold that against you. Not yet. Now—you're following orders from me. Savvy?"

"Me savvy," said his outwitted captive. "Me heap savvy!"

"That's fine," said Gene in a milder tone. "You take down those bars and you pump plenty water for those steers; a little at a time so they don't founder. Savvy?"

The Indian nodded and Gene released him after making sure he had no more instruments of war hidden about his person. Gene swung back into his saddle unaware that Micaela Hardesty was watching him in doe-eyed admiration.

Gene kneed Champ out of the way of the gate and watched the lead steers snuff cautiously at the entrance, then jump across the imaginary line that a gate always made in a steer's mind, into the water pen. The balance of the Boxed H cattle followed close behind and when they were all inside snuffling thirstily in the partly filled troughs, Boomer Banning followed the steers inside with their spare horses, and Gene and Micaela were left alone outside the gate.

Gene was busy putting this latest evidence of Jordan's planning in its proper place while his hands were busy shucking the used cartridge out of the cylinder and slipping another one in its place. How

Jordan would take this interference with his plans
—if they were Jordan's plans and not someone else's
—was something Gene would face when he got to it.
The windmill wrangler didn't have a riding horse
caught up and that meant he couldn't get word to
Jordan right away.

Gene seemed unaware of Micaela's presence until
she sidled her horse closer to him and her pleasant
voice spoke his name. "I suppose you'll be leaving
us, Mr. Autry," she said, and Gene looked at her
and grinned broadly, as he noticed that she had managed to remove most of the dust from her face.

"Why, yes," he said as if surprised at her question. "You won't need a prettied-up dude from here
on in to Hackberry, will you?"

Miss Hardesty flushed and Gene had a sudden
flash of how pretty she could be. Perhaps Micaela
saw this awareness in Gene's eyes, because she waited
a long minute, as if to let him fix her memory in his
mind before she spoke.

"I surely did make a mistake when I cut you in the
dude bunch," she said frankly. "But if we don't need
you from here to Hackberry, I would like to think
that we'll see you when we get there." Micaela
wanted to say "I, I, I," instead of "We," but she
thought it better not to; Mr. Autry might think she
was being a brazen young lady.

Gene looked deep into the brown eyes that gazed
at him and what he saw made him say hurriedly,

"You bet, Miss Hardesty, I'll be sure to see you at Hackberry. Yes indeedy, probably as soon as you get in." He seemed to stop for words, then hastened to add, "I'll have to water Champ and be stepping along. I don't like to push my horse in the heat of day." He gathered up the reins and spoke softly to the horse but Micaela Hardesty's voice stopped him for the third time since they had first met.

"Mr. Autry," she said and her voice was deep with hope and promise, "next time you see me, won't you please call me—" she paused and then smiled like a very little girl, "please call me Micky?"

Gene nodded and rode slowly into the corral to water Champ. When the great horse had slaked his thirst, Gene waved his hand in friendly farewell. One thought ran around and around in his mind, keeping time to Champ's hoofbeats on the trail to Hackberry: *Next time I see her, she may not want me to call her anything.* The girl believed in Jordan's honesty and Gene had ample evidence that she could be stubborn.

# CHAPTER THREE

### JERK-LINE FREIGHTER

The Western States Limited thundered out of Dead Horse Canyon to grind slowly to a stop with a shower of sparks from the protesting brake shoes. The passengers knew the station only as a name in their timetables—Hackberry—and according to the timetables, the Limited stopped ten minutes. The timetables did not see fit to tell the passengers that the stop was made to fill the tender with water for the run across Hualapai Valley to Barstow beyond the Colorado River. The passengers sat inside their luxurious cars and wondered about how this little town came into being.

One of the passengers was too busy to wonder. Calvin Ellicott was making the transcontinental trip alone to visit his grandparents in California. He stood waiting in the vestibule of his sleeping car when the Limited stopped in Hackberry. The porter was reluctant to open the door, but Cal insisted and ran down the steps to the station platform of packed cinders. He was so eager to see everything he could that the porter's friendly warning, "Mind y'all doan get too fur now," went unheeded.

The glimpses from his compartment window as the long train had skirted the town had honed his curiosity to a fine edge. He ran back along the platform beside the cars determined to see everything he could in ten minutes.

A plump little man leaned from an open window in the station beneath the semaphore standard. His shirt sleeves were circled by pink garters with blue bows on them and his cuffs were protected by black sleeve guards. Cal judged him to be the station agent but railroad men held no attraction now.

Lean men in high-heeled boots squatted on their heels against the station wall, and Cal nodded his head in pleasant surprise to see that they looked just like the pictures he had seen back East. Beyond them, a stolid Indian brave stood erect and impassive, and Cal was disappointed that he didn't have the flowing eagle feather headdress he expected. This was something he would have to ask his grandfather about in California. As Cal rounded the end of the station building, his eyes were drawn instantly to the cow ponies hitched to the long peeled cedar pole that was supported by two natural wood forks set deep in the hard ground. Across a dusty street, the buildings of Hackberry fronted the railroad line under a shading row of alamos, whose wind-blown seed pods of fluffy white gave them their common name of cottonwoods.

The street was broad, so broad in fact that the

stream of traffic along it, while respectable enough
for a much larger town than Hackberry, seemed lost
in its expanse. Burros ambled leisurely along, almost
hidden under towering pack loads of camp gear or
merchandise or firewood from the surrounding hills.
Stray dogs went busily about important business of
their own. Riders made their "Sunday horses" show
off their tricks as they came into town. Then, to Cal's
utter delight, a glistening, vermilion varnished,
Concord coach came down the street behind six met-
tlesome black horses.

It was the usual run of daily traffic to Hackberry,
but to Calvin Ellicott, it was the stuff of which his
dreams were made. The train and everything else in
the world was forgotten as he stood on the corner of
the station platform and watched the West parade
before his eyes.

Where he stood, a branch road turned off the
broad main street to cross the railroad tracks and
wind eastward, paralleling the right of way, toward
the black northern peaks of the Sheep Skull Mountains. Down this road came a team of horses. Behind
them, not a wagon, but a second team, then a third,
a fourth, a fifth! Cal raced even farther from his anxious porter and the opened vestibule door to see.

Span by span, a twenty-horse team came down the
road drawing an enormous, high-sided ore wagon.
Behind this wagon was another wagon, hitched by a
short stub of tongue. The driver did not ride the

wagon but sat his saddle on the left-hand horse nearest the wagon, the near wheeler. The coils of a long blacksnake whip were looped over his right shoulder. Instead of multiple reins, like those on the Concord coach, one single line was buckled to the saddle horn and passed forward through rings on the harness of each near horse to the bit in the mouth of the near leader. A slender stick crossed from the near leader's bit to the off leader's. Except for this, the other horses pulled free and unguided; their stretchers taut to the heavy chain that took the place of a wagon tongue on more conventional wagons. From the saddle horn, a wide leather strap led back to the top of the curving brake lever on the lead wagon, a lever ten feet high and as thick as a big man's arm. Cal watched with all his eyes and wished he had two more.

The lead team came to the turn where the road crossed the railroad track to enter Hackberry and Cal's watching eyes saw the driver give two gentle jerks on the long line. The leaders sidestepped to the right, as though they were dancing a polka; the other teams followed, sidewise and forward at the same time being careful to keep wide of the taut chain. The wagons curved majestically around the bend in the road and— The whistle of the Western States Limited as it left the station of Hackberry brought Calvin Ellicott out of his dream world with a gasp of pure dismay.

As he wheeled in frantic haste, the open platform of the observation car seemed to wink scornfully at him as it disappeared around a curve in the track beyond the station. He was suddenly and completely alone.

His clothes, his money, his ticket back home, everything that had made him conscious of being Calvin Ellicott had disappeared in the twinkling of an eye. The broad street of Hackberry with its picturesque traffic, the riders lounging against the station wall, the impassive and immobile Indian, even the wonder of twenty horses pulling two wagons, were no longer fascinating. The sun seemed to beat down on his uncovered head with a new and fierce impact. Calvin's honest, pleasant face began to wrinkle before he could get it under control.

He jammed his hands deep into his trousers pockets while he scuffed one foot idly in the packed cinders of the station platform. What he had to do, said Calvin Ellicott to himself, was to think. And behind his oblivious back, the twenty-horse team and the two big wagons pulled across the railroad tracks and stopped while the sharp-faced man who rode the near wheeler watched the boy with a whimsical expression twisting the corners of his mouth.

Cal didn't get much chance to do his thinking. A heavy hand bit into his shoulder and a coarse raspy voice said, "Whatta yuh doin' around here, you young button?"

Instinctively Cal twisted out of the painful grasp
and faced its owner. What he saw wasn't reassuring.
A thickset body was topped by a chest as big as a
barrel and a squat column of a neck supported a
head that looked as though it had been carved from
a pumpkin. There was no spark of kindliness in the
dull, unwinking, hazel eyes that stared down at Cal,
and the thin-lipped mouth was bordered by two
lines of dried tobacco juice that ran down to lose
themselves in a stubble of dirty whiskers. The only
sign that Cal recognized, he misread completely. On
the left side of the man's soiled vest a five-pointed
star glistened bravely in the sunlight. Cal immediately took heart when he saw it.

"Golly, I'm glad to see you, Officer," said Cal.
"You just must help me."

The tone in his voice would have penetrated any
other man's sensibilities but this man behind the
star was different. One hamlike hand moved idly
sideways, as though brushing off a fly, and Cal went
sprawling on the cinders with his whole face aching
from the blow.

"There," said the man, "thet otta teach yuh to answer muh question. Git up and talk up afore I fetch
you another lick."

The words didn't make any sense to Cal where he
lay dazedly in the sharp cinders. Gone was his sense
of being lost, gone was his desire to have anyone help
him. In their place was a red-hot resentment against

being shoved around by anyone, and a righteous anger that his trust in a man who wore the emblem of the law—Western law—had been betrayed. One knee had been torn out of his trousers and the skinned flesh was raw and throbbing as he rolled over onto his stomach and rose carefully to his hands and knees, digging the toes of his shoes into the cinders for a better purchase. He lifted his head to look up at the man who had struck him with a face streaked with tears—tears of pure anger.

It may have been this evidence that fooled the lawman because he started to step forward and as he did Cal saw his chance to catch him off balance. Cal's head went down and his one hundred and thirty pounds exploded against the man's one solidly planted leg. There was a lot of football practice behind that block and Cal put his whole heart and soul into it. But he was overmatched and bounced off into the cinders.

The lawman staggered off balance and drew back one booted leg with a vicious curse. Cal saw it coming and instead of scrambling like a rabbit to avoid it, he lay where he had fallen and glared up at his tormentor with defiant eyes. The lawman's leg reached its backswing and started down with a terrific force.

Then there was a whistling crack that seemed to jerk that cruel leg right out from under its owner, and his gross body thudded onto the cinders. Cal took quick advantage of this sudden reprieve from danger. He sprang to his feet and took off in full stride, looking earnestly for a rock, for anything to equalize his fight, when a whimsical voice almost directly above him said: "Don't hurt this horse, young fellow, my lad."

Cal's head snapped up and his feet churned wildly when he found himself practically on top of the last horse in the twenty-horse team that had caused him to miss his train. The driver of the team was coiling his long rawhide whip, not hastily, but with a speed that made every motion count. He was smiling a broad, crinkly smile that seemed to lose itself somewhere behind his ears, and Cal was somehow reassured that here was a friend.

The coiling whip and the sudden toppling of the man with the star linked themselves in Cal's mind. He looked up at the man above him and his eyes were wide.

"Did you, did you, did you hit him with that whip?" he blurted.

The broad grin got even broader as the man looked down at his admiring audience. "Just enough," he said, "after you loosened him up." And he and Cal laughed together until Cal's face sobered thoughtfully.

"You know," said Cal, "I think he really would have kicked me."

The man looked down at him and nodded quick

*"Did You Hit Him With That Whip?" Cal Cried*

agreement. "He would have done just that little thing," he said curtly, "and then hauled you off to jail for resisting an officer. He's sudden death if he thinks he can get away with it." His voice suddenly changed tone and timbre. "Look out, son, and watch sharp."

The star-wearer had staggered to his feet, shaking his head like an angry bull. His eyes fastened on Cal standing by the jerk-line team, and he let out a roar as his hand streaked up toward his left armpit. Cal's new-found friend poised his right arm, the coiled whip and handle in it, behind his shoulder and his voice was filled with a flat warning.

"*Quedado hombre!*" he cried, "you, Jordan! Stop it! Or I cut you in two!"

Star Jordan, for it was the marshal of Hackberry himself, stared sullenly at the man with the whip hand, and slowly let his arm fall back by his side.

"Yuh aimin' tuh draw cards in this deal, Wesley?" gritted the discomfited man.

"Mr. Wesley," corrected the man with the whip. "Mr. Pres Wesley, Esquire, jerk-line freighter, tax-payer and honest man alongside the likes of you. I don't aim to draw cards in this deal, I done drawed 'em." He waved the coiled whip ever so slightly to catch Jordan's eye. "And, just in case you got any doubts about it, I'm playing them just as they stand." The coiled whip moved again in reminder.

Star Jordan hunched his heavy shoulders together

almost as though he could feel the whip coiling and curling above them. His sullen face was venomous.

"Yuh talk right sassy," he said, "seein' as how yuh got thuh whip hand."

Mr. Pres Wesley nodded amiably. "Yep," he said, and his drawling voice was pleasant, "I learned how from watching you run roughshod over them that couldn't fight back." Wesley nodded again as if he found the thought well suited to present circumstances.

The marshal's face stayed blank but his eyes never wavered from the coiled whip. Wesley knew that Jordan was biding his time like a coiled rattler. The long whip was heavy to hold indefinitely; one tiny flicker of tired muscles, one instant of relaxed attention, and Jordan's gun would leap from its hide-out. The big marshal was no coward; he just wanted the odds in his favor.

Whatever Wesley was thinking, no tracc of it showed on his weather-beaten face. He eased sideways in his saddle, the better to keep Jordan under domination of his whip, and spoke to the cause of the present trouble.

"Son," said Pres Wesley, "long's you and me are kinda mixed up in the marshal's mind together, what's your name?"

"Calvin Ellicott," replied the boy and he pronounced it "Kolvin."

Wesley's eyes twinkled. "I won't hold that against

you," he said. "I'll call you Calico for short and you can call me Pres. Fair enough?"

Cal looked up at him. Back home he would have resented a name like Calico but on the lips of this man he had known but a few brief minutes, it sounded fine. He grinned his pleasure.

"Now we got that settled," said Pres, "Calico, what on earth were you doing to make the marshal think you were a desperate character?"

The whole sudden sense of his predicament welled up in Cal in response to the warm friendliness of his questioner. The words tumbled out while Pres Wesley sat his horse and his mouth got tighter and tighter with suppressed anger. When Cal was finished, Pres looked at Star Jordan and the disgust in his eyes was a living feeling that even the cold-blooded marshal could understand.

The tension built up and up and up between the two men until Cal felt that something had to happen and his eyes again searched frantically for something to throw if the marshal drew his gun.

A sudden movement by Pres Wesley made the marshal start another stabbing movement toward his armpit hide-out. Cal looked up wildly to see Pres carelessly hanging his whip on his saddle horn. He heard his friend's carefree voice halt the marshal in his tracks with words he could scarcely believe.

"Don't waste a draw, Jordan," said the jerk-line freighter. "Save it for some time when it won't be called just plain murder."

The marshal's sudden movement petered out in puzzled perplexity. Pres looked at his face and chuckled out loud.

"Just over there by the station, Jordan, is a witness to the fact that I am unarmed," said Pres. "None other than the community's leading legal light, Mr. J. Francis Gosslen. You wouldn't want to kill me, or Calico here, in front of a witness, now would you?" The mockery in his voice brought a sullen flush to Star Jordan's stubbled cheeks. "Well," said Pres gaily, "me and Calico'll mosey along. Here, son," he addressed Cal directly, "just slip up behind me on Punch here and we'll go over to Hermie Gerbode's where the air is better."

Cal eagerly slipped his foot into the stirrup that Pres freed for him to use and slid up behind the saddle. As he did, he couldn't resist a last look at his late tormentor. Star Jordan watched them sullenly while toward him across the cinder platform, came J. Francis Gosslen.

He was faultlessly attired in long black frock coat, tight black trousers, snowy shirt of finest linen, black string tie and polished boots of glove-soft leather. A perfectly creased black beaver hat sat squarely atop the Gosslen head and a gold-headed cane of polished ebony twirled slowly in his right hand. It was a right hand that sometimes knew what the left hand did, and neither hand bore the blemishes of hard work. To match this unusual condition, in a country where all men lived by work, generally physical, the Gosslen face was white, stark white, with a black pencil-line mustache to relieve its pallor.

He paused deliberately in front of Star Jordan and looked him up and looked him down, with a cold scorn in his eyes. "You are a perfect specimen of idiot," he said. "Will you never learn that violence is the last resort of fools?"

His voice had a bite in it like a whip, and Jordan again made his instinctive gesture of hitching his powerful shoulders. Gosslen turned on his heel and took his leisurely way toward the main street of Hackberry.

Cal noticed the baffled look on Star Jordan's face as he watched Gosslen's retreating back. It was the look of an over-anxious puppy who has been scolded for doing what he thought was right.

Pres spoke once and the long line of horses expertly took up the slack in the chain, then leaned forward all together and the heavy ore wagons rolled slowly after them.

Pres had his hands full guiding the long line of horses down the street and his mind was busy turning over his responsibility for the boy behind him. Cal had a box seat and not a worry in the world. His eyes flashed from right to left and front and back while he catalogued all the questions that he was sure Mr. Wesley could answer.

Suddenly he grabbed Pres's arm. "Look there, Mr. Wesley," said Cal excitedly pointing to a rider sitting his horse under the shade of a cottonwood. "Isn't that a wonderful sight?"

Pres took in the proud head, the four white feet and the powerful body of the horse. He surveyed the gorgeous saddle and trappings with a practiced eye. Then Pres appraised the rider.

He saw the powerful frame, the frank and honest face, ruggedly handsome, and the well-cut and obviously expensive clothes. His keen eyes caught the way the stranger's gun swung on his hip and the saddle boot that held the rifle. The whole impression was one of a man who was dressed up to lead the Fourth of July parade over in Prescott when they celebrated Frontier Days. It looked like a show and nothing else. But Pres Wesley had lived too long to hang his opinions on just looks.

"Gosh," said Cal in awe, "I wish I had a picture of that horse and his rider."

Pres never took his eyes off Gene and Champ and he noticed that the rider returned his gaze with a level eye. "Calico Cat," said Pres dryly, "that fellow is sure enough duded up to throw a pretty shadow but don't you start judgin' a man by what he wears or says. Men is a whole lot like canned peaches."

"How?" asked Cal quickly.

Pres chuckled. "The label on the can says a lot of things," he said, "but you got to eat the peaches to find out whether the label was lyin' or not. You remember that, Calico Cat."

Cal nodded and kept his eyes fastened on Gene and Champ until the great wagon behind him cut off his view.

# CHAPTER FOUR

## CORRAL DUST

Gerbode's store was the social and financial heart of the Hualapai Valley, the oldest building in Hackberry and the best. One story high, it spread along the main street for a massive solid block with a side street on each side leading back to public feed corrals and stables. The stone foundations on which the floor was built were three feet above the ground. The porch was built on the same level, even with a wagon bed to make loading and unloading easier.

The walls, made of adobe bricks, were four feet thick and fifteen feet high to the ceiling. If you looked closely, you could see loopholes in the walls. These openings, tiny on the outside, widened so that a man indoors by moving his rifle could defend a greater area. Atop the ceiling was a flat roof, cunningly drained against the infrequent gully-washing rains. Above the flat roof, on all four sides, the walls ran up to form a loopholed parapet in times of war. It was Gerbode's store now, and Hackberry's post office, but when Hermic Gerbode built it, it had been Gerbode's Fort as well—a safe haven against the red raiders of Geronimo.

The store itself sprawled along the east side of the building. You asked for what you wanted and it was handed to you over the counter, or fished down from its resting place on the cedar *vigas* that supported the heavy roof. No storage space was wasted for Hermie Gerbode boasted that he could sell you anything from a five-stamp quartz mill to a paper of pins and he could. Under the same sheltering roof, the Hackberry Hotel took up the western part of the building and, sandwiched between store and hotel, was the best eating place in Hackberry. Hermie Gerbode set a good table. A door opened from store to dining-room and from hotel to dining-room, with a door off the loading platform porch into each establishment.

In the apparently disordered space of the store itself, one tiny corner was partitioned off in brick. Its brave window was plate glass, sparkling in the sun and spotlessly clean. Gold letters spelled a message across the window.

BANK OF HACKBERRY

*H. Gerbode, Pres.*

Across the street, a squat adobe with iron-barred windows dominated a scattered row of buildings. A sign above the side door bore the legend—*Town Marshal.*

Some of these things Cal saw as the two wagons drew to a halt against the platform porch of Gerbode's store. The horses let the chain fall slack, Pres Wesley eased himself in the saddle and Hermie Gerbode bustled out to meet him; short and fat with a halo of snow-white hair frizzling up in all directions. Freighter and merchant shook hands warmly.

"Well, Hermie," said Pres, "I hope you got some willing hands to load this ore on the car. I don't want to do it all, all alone."

Gerbode grunted. "Ach! dere iss no gar yet. Rodden service py der railroad. It should haff pin here yesterday already. Trive py der veed gorrel, Bres. Unhidtch unt veed. Mine expense, off goarse, until I can your vagons unloat."

"I can take out on the flats," said Pres. "Make camp and hobble 'em, if you have to wait for your car. Feeding twenty horses will cost you money, Hermie, and there's lots of free grass or—" His voice trailed off in a question.

"Or doss harness cost more yet as veed?" supplied Hermie. "You know der answer, Bres. Dey'd steal der harness, horses, vaggons, ore unt all if der chanct came. It iss not like old times." He shook his head sadly.

Pres nodded silently. "Can do, Hermie," he said. "There'll be no charge for the wagons while I'm waiting. You paying for the feed is plenty and, besides," he laughed, "I'm not business man enough to make a profit out of your hard luck not getting a car to load your ore soon's I got in."

Gerbode bobbed his head in appreciation. "It is still old times to do pizness mitt you, Bres," he said.

Pres smiled warmly at his old friend. "I see you got the window all dolled up," he said. "When will you be ready to let me borry enough to enjoy myself?"

Hermie looked around him cautiously. "Comes it tomorrow morning der bank ge opens yet," he whispered. "Broviding, of goarse, dat ve are ready. I know later on."

"Be a fine thing whenever you do open, Hermie," said Pres seriously. "Folks can get a square deal from the bank 'thout goin' to that penny pinchin' Gosslen."

Gerbode bobbed his head vigorously. "Yah, Bres, ve giff a square deal always," he said. "Undt dott Baca, he puts his name py mine on der bapers for der insurance when der bank is officially for pusiness ready. He is vun fine man, py gollys!"

"Is 'Relio in town?" asked Pres in surprise.

"Nod yed," said Hermie, "put he comes tonight from der ranch." A voice called from inside the store. "Excuse, Bres," said Hermie and hustled inside to satisfy his customer.

The great wagons rolled out from the porch platform of Gerbode's Store, curved around the corner of that massive building, and came to a stop in the wagonyard behind the feed corrals. Cal jumped down from his seat behind Pres's saddle and when Pres himself was on the ground, Cal faced him with shining eyes and burst into talk.

"I would not have missed it for anything, Mr. Wesley," he cried.

"The name is Pres," came the firm reminder. "Pres and Calico, remember?" and the firmness was softened by twinkling eyes.

"Certainly, I remember," Cal replied. "I just forgot. There are so many things I want to ask you. About freighting and how you manage twenty horses and how you train them and how much can you haul and how far and what the ore is worth and—" He paused for breath. "Did you hear me, Mr. — I mean, Pres?"

Pres kept his face straight with an effort. "Yes, Calico, I heard you; at least I think I did before you got excited. Now you pay heed to what your Uncle Pres tells you." Cal looked up at him with expectancy. "You just use your eyes and your brain as fast as you use your tongue, Calico, and —" There was a long pause.

"And what?" said Cal in a hurry. He had just thought of some more questions.

"Why you'll learn nearly anything you want to know without plaguing Uncle Pres," was the laughing retort.

Cal's crestfallen face moved Pres to say, "Never mind, Calico. We'll unhitch a span at a time and unharness as we go. You'll learn lots before we're through."

Twenty horses were unharnessed and watered,

fed with good grama grass hay and nubbly ears of
Indian corn, and Cal had learned a lot. The names
of twenty horses, from Punch and Judy, the wheel-
ers, to Tom and Jerry, the lead team; how the swing
team hopped the chain on short curves and pulled
at almost right angles to the pull of the chain itself;
how the trail wagon was dropped in heavy going and
then coupled on again; how the chuck box on the
tail gate of the trail wagon got its name and how it
worked; it was a great and wonderful lesson for Cal.
And when Pres gave him a currycomb and brush to
work over the sweat-caked shoulders of Punch and
Judy, he felt that he was really lending his friend a
hand.

Pres was still imparting precious bits of information to Cal when a chorus of shouts and laughter
came from a smaller corral outside the feed stalls.
One of the stablemen passed by and Pres called out
familiarly, "Hi, what's going on in the other corral?"

"Some fellow's goin' to top a bronc that Jordan
just bought," was the indifferent reply.

"Calico Cat," said Pres firmly, "you ever seen a
bronc topped off?"

Cal shook his head.

"Come on then," said Pres. "I better complete
your education before you catch the Limited tomorrow; and you remind me to send your folks in California a telegram so's they won't worry none."

Pres climbed the corral fence and settled himself

comfortably on the board that made a flat railing atop the highest bar. Cal quickly followed suit. A laughing group of men shouted encouragement to a horse and jeering advice to a sandy-haired man who stood apart from the group in silent study of the horse. The men held no interest for Cal right then. His eyes were riveted on the horse, and with good reason.

The horse was powerfully built and short coupled. His curving, alert ears pointed at the man who studied him and his eyes seemed almost human. What really claimed Cal's interest was his color. Head, neck, and forequarters were a deep and glistening golden brown. This solid color stopped short at the rounded muscular rump and was replaced by a startling pattern of hair mottled with deep-red, egg-shaped spots. Cal thought it looked as if someone had draped a sheet over the horse's hindquarters and thrown ripe tomatoes at it. Another oddity was its hoofs. They were striped vertically in black and white. Cal had never seen a horse like this. He was so absorbed in his study that he forgot to ask Pres any questions.

Pres gave the horse a quick look as soon as he topped the corral fence but his chief attention was on the men gathered in the corral. On the far side, standing by the gate, stood Star Jordan flanked by several hard-eyed *buscaderos* from his Ladder outfit. There was a coarse-grained grin on Jordan's face and

Pres didn't like the looks of it.

Several townspeople and railroad men sat on the corral fence to the right of the stout gateposts. A little apart from them roosted a couple of city-dressed men whom Pres took to be "drummers" from their plump pink faces and pudgy hands. The lone man standing almost beneath his feet was Johnny Hines, and Pres wondered what had caused him to get mixed up with Jordan and the Ladders.

Pres carefully pried a sliver from the corral railing and began to whittle long shavings that curled off to flutter down at Johnny's feet. The sandy-haired puncher looked up quickly. His freckled face relaxed into a grin when he saw Pres Wesley.

"Hi, Old Rawhider," he cried out. "How'd you get way up there? Somebody push you from behind?"

Pres grinned down at Johnny. "That's always the way with you young bucks," he said slowly. "Thinking anybody that's got brains enough not to ride broncs needs a nursemaid or one of them sassiety folks' valleys. How come you let yourself get mixed up with this shivvaree? Workin' for Jordan?" Pres grinned more broadly.

"Not any, nohow," said Johnny. "Just couldn't keep my big yap closed."

"That's chronic with you," was Pres's dry comment. "What happened?"

"Oh, nawthin'," said Johnny. "I just come amblin' into town to see if it was still here. While I was

checkin' my gun at Hermie's, Jordan jumps me to
ride this bronc of his'n. Claims it's never been rode
and done throwed all the Ladder hands what
climbed on him. I just listened."

"Did you feel bad?" asked Pres.

"Not right away." Johnny grinned. "Thet may
come later—after I forks him."

"You're goin' to ride him," said Pres incredulous-
ly, "and for Jordan to boot. Thought you and him
weren't *simpatico*."

"Ain't," grunted Johnny. "But when Jordan shot
off his big mouth about nobody being able to ride
this horse after his Texas gunnies got throwed, I bet
him five large round dollars that little old Johnny
Hines was the man to do it. Here I am," he went on,
"and there's the horse. The more I look at him, the
more I figure I'm really gonna earn my money."

"That's all right, Johnny," said Pres consolingly.
"There has to be a first time for everything. I'll buy
you some arniky."

Johnny snorted his disdain for all medicines and
resumed his careful study of the queerly spotted
horse. Pres felt an impatient tugging at his sleeve and
turned to face a wide-eyed and breathless Cal.

"Pres, what gives that horse such a queer color
and where did he come from and why are his feet
striped that way and what will he do when that man
gets on him and—" His headlong rush was checked
by Pres's drawling exclamation.

"Whoa, now, whoa, now," said Pres. "You keep your eyes open and you'll find out what he does when Johnny Hines straddles him. Now, that's one answered."

Cal rushed ahead. "But you still haven't told me all the rest, about where he came from and why that funny coloring and about his feet and everything else," he begged.

Pres took a deep deliberate breath until he saw that Cal was about to twist off the corral fence in impatience.

"Calico Cat," said Pres, "that's an appaloosa horse from up in Idaho. The Nez Perce Indians have raised his kind ever since they got horses from the Spaniards." His mind revolved the thought as if he were looking backward across the years. "That's a long time ago," he went on. "Those Indians heap savvied what they wanted a horse to be and to look like. They kept selecting horses that had these queer color patches and they kept them apart from the rest of their *manadas* until they had a breed all their own. Those hoofs got that way from the same reason. That white in them is tougher and more stretchy than rubber. The black is harder than flint rock. Horses need hoofs that can take punishment up in the lava brakes along the Snake River."

Cal didn't seem convinced. "Pres," he said in a small, doubtful voice, "you aren't just making that up, are you?"

Pres caught the fear of misplaced confidence in Cal's voice. "Calico," he said, "Pres Wesley wouldn't run a windy on you even if he could. What makes you think I'm makin' it up?"

Cal seemed a little sheepish that he had suspected Pres but he had to go through with it now. "Well, it just doesn't seem possible," he groped for his words and then blurted out, "that those Indians would have been intelligent enough to do it the way you said."

"Calico, don't you ever get the idea that Indians don't have brains," Pres said firmly. "They got plenty of 'em. Only thing is they don't talk about it as much as some other color skins I could name. No, sir, Calico Cat," he said, "when the Army finally corraled Chief Joseph, the peace treaty made the Nez Perce surrender exactly one thousand of these spotted *caballos* so the white man could get the benefit of them. That proves they're good horses, don't it?"

Cal nodded. Then he looked up at Pres with a determined glint in his eyes. "I'm sorry I doubted you, Pres," he said, "but I'm glad I learned the story."

A pleased look spread across Pres's face. "You done just right, Calico Cat," said Pres. "If you don't believe something, you sure ought to speak your piece. You did just that and you had gumption enough to admit you was wrong."

The way he said it made Cal feel warm all over

inside. Pres was talking to him man to man.

He was about to ask Pres another question when a sudden flurry of excitement in the corral made them both look. Johnny Hines had carefully looped the horse with the quick underarm throw of a skilled roper, and swiftly snubbed the rope to a stout cedar post in the center of the corral. The horse bawled in fright at the unaccustomed noose tight around his neck. Johnny soothed him with his voice until the horse stood still at the end of the rope, head up, nostrils wide and whistling, trembling in every muscle. Johnny watched him for several minutes, still soothing him with his low reassuring voice, and then Johnny started walking over toward the corral gate.

Pres followed him with his eyes and noticed that a newcomer was perched on the corral fence to the left of the gate. It was J. Francis Gosslen. The way he sat there clasping his cane between his knees, reminded Pres of an undertaker visiting a sick man. Johnny was almost to the gate when one of the Ladder men by Jordan's side spoke out in a loud, sneering voice.

"Welshin' on thet bet, Hines?" he asked, the tone more of an insult than the words.

Johnny's fists clenched at his sides, but his voice was under control. "I can cover any bet you want to make before I get my saddle," he answered.

The Ladder man laughed hoarsely and moved forward a step, his arms curving down toward his

*Johnny Soothed the Horse With His Voice*

hips. Star Jordan stopped him with a gesture and spoke to Johnny in as pleasant a voice as he could manage.

"If it's a saddle yore after, yuh can take thet one there," said Jordan, pointing to a double rigged hull resting against the side of the corral. "Them stirrups is just about yore length. But mebbe yuh better not," he went on, "I shore don't want yuh tuh have no excuse fer gittin' throwed."

Jordan chuckled at the prospect and Johnny's face clouded in anger. The marshal saw it and spoke again. " 'Course, I plumb forgot thet a real Texas man's saddle might made yuh oncomfortable," he said, tauntingly.

Johnny's quick temper boiled up inside him but he figured he could best Jordan in any way, even with words.

"Well, now," said Johnny Hines, and his slow even drawl was unexpectedly polite, "I never needed two cinches before but I guess I'll take you up on that saddle, just so's it'll always know how it feels to have an honest man sit in it." He grinned impudently at Jordan and his gunmen, and picked up the saddle.

Pres didn't like the way things were shaping up. Johnny Hines ought to know better than to use a saddle of Jordan's. He was on the point of calling a warning to Johnny when Cal's low whistle of delight claimed his attention.

The big sorrel horse and his rider had ridden up to the corral fence and now Gene was standing easily on top of his saddle for a better look at what was going on inside the corral. His face concealed whatever thoughts ran through his mind as he watched Johnny step into the trap he had set for himself.

The bronc was standing at the extreme end of the rope that held him to the snubbing post. He snorted wildly as Johnny came down the line toward him, talking all the time, almost crooning. There was a flurry of movement from the horse as Johnny put out his hand toward the flaring nostrils. Slowly, patiently, Johnny patted the velvet nose, then slid his hand upward to rub the dark head between the ears. Slowly, ever so slowly, without a hasty move or a sign of fear, Johnny slipped on the jaquima. Gently he placed the saddle blanket on the nervously wrinkling back after the hackamore was secure.

The spotted horse snorted and humped his back. The blanket slid to the ground. Johnny displayed no annoyance as he carefully replaced the blanket and with quick sureness slid the borrowed saddle onto the blanket and threaded the latigos through the cinch rings. Johnny slowly tightened the cinches and the firmness of his actions plus the soothing cadence of his voice seemed to mesmerize the bronc. Johnny was singing to himself and to the frightened horse. *"Next comes my saddle an' I screws her down tight. I steps aboard him and raises the blind, I'm right in his middle to see him unwind."*

"Of course, old spotty," said Johnny to the horse, "I don't have no blinds on you 'cause we won't need 'em, you just wait and see. Why, shuckins, horse, this ain't goin' to hurt us none atall, atall." As he spoke, Johnny grasped the hackamore, eased his left foot into the near stirrup and flowed up into the saddle. His foot found the off stirrup and as it did, he broke into the last verse of his favorite song. *"An' I'll bet all my money thet the man ain't alive what kin ride ol' strawberry when he takes his high dive."*

Johnny settled himself and looked directly at the man standing in the saddle of the great sorrel horse outside the corral. Not a flicker of recognition passed between them but Johnny felt a whole lot better to know Gene was there.

As Johnny eased himself aboard the bronc, Pres's voice came clearly to Gene's ears. "Calico Cat," said Pres, "you done seen a pretty job of handlin' a bronc for the first time. That Johnny Hines sureleee can speak their language. No muss, fuss or hellity-larrup slam-bang horse-breakin' that leaves you nothin' but a cold-jawed plug." He nodded his head violently and Gene inwardly agreed with this man's summation. Johnny Hines could handle broncs a whole lot better than he could handle himself. Gene watched the next move from Johnny with wary attention. That borrowed saddle was bad medicine in his opinion.

Johnny slid the snubbing rope up and over the twitching ears and let it slide to the ground. He slowly tightened the hackamore reins and patted the bronc's quivering neck. "Come on, horse," said Johnny mildly. "Step out once. C-chk! C-chk!" The bronc took a cautious sidewise step. It didn't hurt him. He took another step, then another and another, while Johnny's voice reassured him it was all right.

"Go git him, hawse," yelled one of the Ladder men with Jordan and scaled his big black sombrero between the bronc's legs. The spotted horse fairly screamed with fright as he went up, up, up into the air, to swap ends and come down bawling, bucking across the corral toward Gene. Johnny rode easily for one jump, then another, then another—on the fourth jump, saddle and man left the bronc's back together and rolled in the dust almost beneath his plunging feet.

The appaloosa sprang high in the air while Johnny scrambled dazedly to escape the next downward plunge of his bunched feet. A six-gun barked once as Gene sprang from Champ's back to the fence and into the corral before the report was understood by the onlookers. Gene was on top of the bronc when he hit and lay still; he snapped the snubbing rope around the horse's neck and was satisfied with the results of his shot, clearly visible between the horse's ears.

He rolled the saddle over toward Johnny and hastily rolled Johnny against the saddle. His voice was a crisp undertone. "You almost picked a harp for yourself, Johnny my lad," said Gene. "Those cinches was cut darn near through. Johnny, you sure stepped into it. Now make it look good." This last order was uttered as he stepped quickly away from the reclining Johnny.

"Take your hands offen me," yelled Johnny so all could hear. "I don't need no dressed-up dude pawin' me around. I ain't hurt and I don't want my pocket picked. Go on, leave me alone." He glared at Gene who shrugged his shoulders and started toward the fence.

"Who pulled thet gun?" bellowed Star Jordan, "Who did it?" The marshal and his men had not stirred from their positions against the corral fence to help Johnny out of trouble but now they moved slowly toward him.

Gene turned slowly in his tracks and looked at the approaching group. He sniffed the air as if it were suddenly tainted. "You must be what passes for the law around here," said Gene in a curious tone. Jordan scowled and said nothing. "I can't understand it," said Gene, he seemed to be talking to himself but his voice carried, "here's a boy just missed getting tromped to death and the law doesn't make a move to stop it. Then it yaps and yells about guns." He shook his head in bewilderment.

Jordan lumbered toward Gene and a fearsome scowl contorted his heavy face. "Yoh're wearin' a gun," he growled, "lessee it!"

Gene shook his head. "Nooooh," he drawled, "I keep it. If you want to see it, you can look at it this way." His handsome six-shooter flashed into his hand as if from thin air and was back in its holster before the marshal and his men could believe their eyes. "I've been moving a whole lot just recently," said Gene, "and I kinda hoped Hackberry would be my kind of town. I was wrong, plumb wrong," said Gene. "I can smell how wrong I was without straining my nose." He sniffed the air and made a wry face.

Jordan hunched his heavy shoulders. "Yore mighty free with yore tongue, pretty boy," he snarled.

"Mebbe I am," said Gene with a rising note in his voice, "but I'm not half so free with my tongue as somebody is with their knife."

"Whattuh yuh drivin' at?" rasped Jordan.

"You look at the saddle you flim-flammed that rider into using," said Gene slowly. "The off latigos were cut where they double over the cinch rings. Which one of you sidewinders did it?" Gene's voice was heavy with contempt.

Jordan seemed to grasp the implications of Gene's word with a slow rage. A baffled, frustrated snarl curled from his lips and he made an instinctive gesture toward his shoulder gun. The Ladder men behind him reached for their personal hardware and Gene balanced on the balls of his feet and waited.

Suddenly a clear, cold voice hit Jordan like a bucket of snow water. "You are over-hasty, Marshal," said the voice and Jordan wheeled to face it in gaping amazement. "Yes," continued J. Francis Gosslen, "I am sure of it. You must have accused the wrong man."

"But—but—but who kilt muh horse?" rumbled the puzzled Jordan.

"A party or parties unknown," said Gosslen smoothly. "There were several spectators sitting on the fence as you should remember. They are not here now as even you can see. It was one of them, I think. Don't you agree, Marshal Jordan?" There was a cutting edge to Gosslen's voice, a tone of command.

Gene's trained ear caught the difference in tone and he wondered at it. He wondered, too, why this somberly dressed man had diverted the marshal's attention. Gene played it close to his chest and said nothing. Watching and listening were the pay-off tricks right now.

Jordan's face was a study in displeasure as he turned slowly to look at Gene. "Guess I was wrong," he said ungracefully.

Gene acknowledged this courtesy by turning on his heel and lithely swinging up and over the fence into the saddle on Champ's waiting back. He regarded Jordan with a stony indifference.

Jordan turned his attention to Johnny Hines who still reclined against the treacherous saddle. "Yuh didn't ride thet bronc," he said thickly, "Yuh kin pay me thet five dollars yuh lost."

Johnny didn't pay any attention to Jordan or the men behind him. He was staring intently at a red-clotted spot on the appaloosa's head, where the head-stall crossed behind its ears.

Jordan growled sullenly and raised his voice. "Yuh pays me thet bet," rasped Jordan menacingly, "and fer the hawse too."

Johnny slowly lifted his head as if he didn't want to look at what he knew was there. He got to his feet and braced himself on wide-spraddled legs.

Gene had seen Johnny plant himself this way before and he hoped Johnny would keep his head.

"I feel real bad about losing the five you'd have owed me if me and thet bronc had been left alone," said Johnny deceptively. "What really gravels me is that poor bronc. Him and me were gettin' along just fine, Jordan." Johnny seemed to remember how fine they had been making out together. "Yessir," said Johnny, "that bronc was tryin' his best to understand and it wasn't his fault that he didn't get the chance. Somebody sailed a great big hat at him." Johnny's face took on an angelic smile. "I don't pay you no five dollars, Jordan, and I don't pay you for no horse neither. Why don't you let him that caused the trouble pay for it? Who's bareheaded, Jordan?"

The last question crackled like cold bacon in a hot skillet.

The bareheaded man was Boy Nolan, Jordan's straw-boss, a gunman with a hard-case reputation. "I didn't mean no harm," he muttered. "Jes' wanted tuh see if Hines could make a ride. Where's my hat anyhow?"

Johnny pointed a finger. "It just must be under thet bronc it scared so bad," he said gleefully.

Nolan swore viciously. "Thet was a new hat," he raved. "If it's tromped or cut up, you redheaded peckerwood, I'll have blood for it."

"You shuck thet gun you're supposed to be so careless with," said Johnny tightly, "an' you can start getting blood. It'll be yours and all over you, you snake-eyed hyena."

Nolan snatched at his gun belt like a man in haste to get rid of it and Jordan stopped him with an oath. Then he turned to Johnny. "Yuh're lookin' fer trouble, Hines," he said.

"Mebbe I am," said Johnny wrathfully. He grasped the saddle behind him and twisted it angrily around to Jordan's feet. "I heard that show-off dude throw cinch-cutting right in your faces and you never bobbled. Look there," cried Johnny, "and you can see them cut. I can lick any or all of you that done it." Johnny's voice was filled with contempt for the men who had tried to murder him in an underhanded way. The fact that he had walked right

into the trap simply made him madder. Johnny lost
all remembrance of the mission that Gene had to ac-
complish in Hackberry and his part in the drama was
forgotten completely. Johnny started toward Jordan
with the whole-souled and simple desire to smash
him with his fists.

Jordan hunched his heavy shoulders and waited.
Hines was walking right into certain death and Jordan would make sure that he didn't escape this time.
Johnny had taken but one step forward when a whistling rawhide noose dropped over his head and
snapped tight around his chest and arms with pinioning force. Champ exerted the steady backward
pull of the skillful rope horse and Gene's riata dal-
lied around the saddle horn, pulled Johnny Hines
out of danger with a remorseless force. Jordan was
deprived of his excuse to kill an unarmed man on
the pretext that he had been threatened.

Jordan's face reflected the slow thought process of
his mind. Pres watched Johnny's backward progress
with a look of respect for the pretty-shadow stranger
on his face. Cal learned a lot of new words as Johnny
struggled to escape the pinioning riata and J. Francis
Gosslen nursed his cane between two bony knees
and concealed his thoughts behind his heavy-lidded
and pallid face.

Gene pulled Johnny snug against the corral fence
and signaled Champ with his knees. Champ leaped
forward and the riata seemed to recoil itself auto-

matically in Gene's left hand. Before Johnny realized it, Champ's head was over the corral fence and
Gene was looking down at him.

"I'll take my loop now," said Gene. "That is, if
you're finished with it."

Johnny snatched the loop over his head and threw
it in the dirt. "It don't take no guts to rope a man
from behind," he yelled. "Get off that hobby-horse,
you grandstanding dude, and I'll clean your plow
just to get warmed up for Jordan."

Gene smiled a fatherly smile at the irate Johnny.
"I might just accommodate you," he said, "but I
promised myself not to play Special Divine Provi-
dence more than twice in the same day. You remember that," said Gene, almost gently.

"I don't need no rodeo parade rider to help me
out," barked Johnny. "You leave me and my problems alone and we'll both live longer. You savvy that
talk? Or do I have to crawl over this fence and bat it
into you?"

Gene just grinned and Johnny flushed a deeper
shade of red. He had forgotten everything in his un-
thinking, instinctive anger at Jordan and now he
directed the heat of his passions at Gene. His face
worked with temper but before he could give it
words, a clatter of hoofs pounded up to the corral
gate.

"Hey, Star," cried a loud voice, "yuh're wanted
*muy pronto.*" The man rode a Ladder horse.

"Whut's thuh matter?" growled the marshal. "Shootin' scrape or a drunk raisin' a ruction?"

"Worse'n thet," said the rider. "There's a girl and a waspy old geezer over to the railroad stawkyards, with a little bunch o' steers. Girl done watered 'em and when thuh station agent tried tuh collect a charge like yuh tol' him, the old geezer stuck his rifle in thuh agent's belly and the agent begun sayin' prayers and hollerin' blue murder. I heerd him and rode past. He acts like he wants you quick."

Gene watched Jordan and his men stump awkwardly over to the gate in their high-heeled boots to get their horses while he filed the chance remark about the station agent taking Jordan's instructions for future reference. He looked again at Johnny who gave him a baleful stare and turned his back to speak loudly to Pres on the opposite side of the corral.

"Guess I'll get my horse and mosey over toward the stockpens, Pres," said Johnny. "Want to side me?"

Pres shook his head. "I heard that Ladder jasper say there was a girl over there, Johnny," he laughed. "I always like to give you first chance. Not that it ever does you any good."

Johnny shrugged his shoulders resignedly. "I just naturally hate to cut you out every time," he said, "but if you're too ornery to take advantage of my kind nature, thet's up to you. Just don't come snuffin' aroun' when I escorts her to the evenin' meal tonight." Johnny took his leave with an airy wave of his hand.

Gene watched him go and swung down from his saddle to watch the appaloosa bronc through the corral fence. He was conscious of an excited voice asking hurried questions of Pres Wesley but his attention was riveted on the bronc still so motionless in the dust. Suddenly, Gene saw a quiver of nervous muscles ripple across the appaloosa's neck. The proud head tried to lift itself from the dust only to flop down again. Another head-lifting and another, each one stronger than the last, was followed by a frantic beating of hoofs as the bronc struggled to get his forefeet under him. Gene heard the excited voice across the corral pitch upward.

"Pres, Pres, just look," said Cal. "He isn't really dead. Let's help him." He tried to jump down into the corral and Gene saw Pres grab him with a strong hand.

"You may be able to jar Jordan off balance," laughed Pres, "but that horse is too much. Let him alone and watch him."

Pres and Cal were so engrossed in the spectacle of the dead horse coming back to life that they failed to notice the movements of J. Francis Gosslen. Gene saw him and swung back into the saddle.

The lively struggles of the appaloosa apparently moved Mr. Gosslen to action. He descended from his perch on the fence, dusted his hands with a hand-

*"The Bronc Isn't Dead!" Said Cal*

kerchief plucked from his sleeve cuff and walked deliberately around the corral to where Gene sat Champ as if they were both cast from the same bronze mold.

The Gosslen eye was calm and the Gosslen face was blank. His voice was bland and flattering. "Permit me to congratulate you on the ability to use your brains before using those beautiful weapons you carry," purred J. Francis Gosslen. "I must also congratulate you on the excellence of your aim. I would not have believed it possible." He paused and looked up at Gene with a cynical smile. "Perhaps Hackberry will be to your liking," he said and picked his way on around the corral toward the railroad station.

Gene watched him go without a sign on his face and he felt an inward loathing of this cold-blooded person who dealt in double meanings when he spoke. Gene gave his attention to the corral with a feeling of relief. The appaloosa was on his feet and when he saw Gene, he snorted and ran to the end of the rope on wobbly knees. Gene saw that a few minutes more would make him as good as new except for an unaccustomed soreness between his ears. He was about to signal Champ to ride away, when Cal's excited voice made him halt his intention.

"Why wasn't that horse dead, Pres," he asked, "and who fired that shot and why did somebody cut Mr. Hines's cinch and could he really lick that Star Jordan and can we see the herd at the stockyards if we go out now and—"

"Whoa now, Calico Cat," reminded Pres. "You ask 'em one at a time and I'll try to answer them. Now then, let me make a think." He whittled a match for what must have been an eternity to Cal and Gene had the impression that Pres was trying to collect his thoughts for more ears than just Cal's.

"Calico Cat," said Pres too loudly, "we will hence-forth, forthwith and wherefor, take up the matter of your incurable curiosity. Those cinches were cut with the fond hope that J. Johnny Hines would come to a sudden and unpleasant end with malice afore-thought."

"Why?" asked Cal, "and how did they know he would use it?"

"The why is because Jordan wants what Johnny owns, Spur Spring, and Johnny won't be scared off. If a bronc tromps him, it looks legal as all get out. They didn't know he'd use thet saddle but they hoped he would and somebody besides that pot-bel-lied marshal savvied how to make Johnny use it."

"Who?" asked Cal.

"Dunno," said Pres, "and it bothers me. I never did like to admit I was ignorant. Now lessee," he pretended to count off Cal's questions on his fingers. "Oh, yes, why wasn't that horse dead? That horse wasn't dead because he'd been creased between the ears with a six-shooter bullet. And, Calico Cat," said Pres earnestly, "you can tell your grandchildren that you saw it done. That bullet just grazed the skull enough to stun that bronc and save Johnny Hines's ungrateful carcass. It's the hardest shot in the world and the man who did it—why, son, he had every- thing it takes plus a lot of confidence in himself."

"But that clergyman on the fence said—" began Cal, and Pres snorted.

"Don't ever mistake J. Francis Gosslen for no clergyman," said Pres. "I don't know why he said what he did, and I'm apt to lay awake nights puz- zling it out, but none of them railroaders or them drummers could make a crease shot."

"Who did?" asked Cal impatiently.

Pres smiled a knowledgeable smile. "Your self- appointed Uncle Pres will make you a good freehand guess that there's one empty cartridge in that cylin- der of your pretty-shadow stranger's gun," said Pres, and he looked directly at Gene to see if the guess went home. Gene deliberately drew his gun and punched the empty shell into his hand. Then he dropped the empty into his shirt pocket and calmly stuffed a fresh cartridge into the cylinder. He gave no sign that he had heard Pres's guess or that he was at all concerned by Pres's speculative gaze.

"But, Pres," sputtered Cal, "you call him pretty- shadow and Mr. Hines called him a whole lot of names. How could he make a shot like that?"

"Calico Cat," said Pres, "Johnny Hines was hasty in his talk and he didn't have no likin' for being

pulled off Jordan like a calf bein' weaned. You remember what I told you about that label on the
peach can?"

Cal nodded.

"You keep right on rememberin' it," said Pres.
"Come on, son, let's *pasear* over to the stockpens."

Gene lifted the bridle reins and Champ single-
footed toward the stockyards where the Boxed H
herd was having more trouble over watering charges.
The rungs in the ladder were slowly being climbed
and Gene felt confident of reaching the top a whole
lot quicker than he had thought before the incident
in the corral.

# CHAPTER FIVE

## RAILROADED

The railroad stockyards were designed to hold big herds of wild cattle, or wilder horses. Tough cedar posts a foot in diameter and ten feet tall held heavy whipsawed planks that were a foot wide and half that thick. One main pen enclosed the water troughs, a pen that could hold a thousand head of long-horned cattle. Gates and runways led from it to smaller pens, and these in turn led into separate chutes that enabled three stock cars to be loaded simultaneously. The stockyards were there for the use of the cattlemen who shipped over the cars of the Pacific Railroad. They were a vital part of the great commerce of range cattle into meat for the nation. Now, they were a trap for the Boxed H steers who drank eagerly inside the main pen. And they were a trap for the owner of those steers even though she stood outside the stockyard gate.

Gene rode slowly around the rim of the stockyards toward the main gate and his nerve ends tingled as he sized up the situation. A Ladder hand lounged against the closed main gate, holding a familiar short barreled carbine. Two other Ladder men held a glaring Banning, shorn of his rifle. A pot-bellied little man in a green eye shade with offensively pink garters around his sleeves massaged the pit of his stomach while he voiced loud complaints to Marshal Jordan who stood near Micky Hardesty.

"Marshal," he sputtered, "I want you to know that I was forced to open these stockyards at the point of a deadly weapon." He rubbed his stomach as if in memory. "It's just your timely arrival that prevented me from being killed. That rifle might have gone off." He seemed to flinch at the thought.

Banning struggled helplessly in the pinioning arms that held him. "Wisht it had of," he said balefully.

"You hear that, Marshal?" cried the agent, his eye shade bobbing for punctuation marks. "He's a desperate character. I demand protection in safeguarding railroad property—and my life," he added.

Jordan nodded. "Yuh got any more complaints tuh make?" he asked hopefully.

"Yes, I have," said the station agent. "I want that herd impounded by the law until the watering charges are paid. Dollar a head, cash." He rubbed his hands together vindictively.

Gene couldn't believe his ears! No railroad in its right mind ever charged cattlemen for watering their livestock. Freight charges on cattle were the railroad's life blood. If they antagonized the cowmen, they wouldn't get the business. The Santa Fe line wasn't too far away and the Santa Fe was a tough competitor. It didn't make sense and Gene knew there was something sinister behind this move.

Jordan nodded solemnly toward the station agent. "If yuh says so," he said, "I guess I'll have tuh see thet it's collected." He turned to Micky, whose face reflected her utter dismay. "I shore hates tuh do it, Miss Hardesty," said Jordan, shaking his head, "but I got tuh enforce thuh law iffen he asks me tuh."

"I don't have that much cash," said Mickey. She seemed to stiffen with a new thought. "Besides," she said, "it's plain ridiculous. Whoever heard of a railroad charging for water when cattle are waiting to be shipped in their cars? Why didn't you tell me about this when you sent me that message to ship my steers in Hackberry?"

Jordan's heavy face seemed genuinely embarrassed. "Miss Hardesty," he said, "it shore don't seem reasonable but I got tuh do it iffen the agent asks me." He seemed almost relieved. "You heard him tell me, didn't you?"

Micky nodded.

"No'm," said Jordan, "I shore don't cotton tuh it, but I got tuh." He paused as if thinking up something to make himself look better in the eyes of this attractive girl. Jordan could see that he'd made a real good move when he had asked her to come to Hackberry.

"Yuh see, Miss Hardesty," he said ingratiatingly, "this here's a new regulation. They caught me with it just yestiddy." He laughed falsely at the good joke on himself. "Thuh boys brung a big bunch of my Ladder stock in tuh wait fer thuh buyer and thuh agent done charged me fer watering jest like he's doin' now. Goin' to be some expensive iffen I have tuh hold my herd out on thuh flats and water 'em here every day till thet buyer shows up."

"What do you mean?" asked Micky and her voice was anguished. "You told me a buyer would be waiting here!"

Jordan seemed at a loss for words. He twisted his hat in one hand and with the other one, he reached out and grasped Micky's ungloved hand. "Now don't yuh git excited," he soothed. "I shore thought there'd be a buyer here when yuh showed up. I did so. But I had a telegram from him this mawnin' that he done stopped over in Peach Springs tuh look at some TO steers. I don't like it no better'n yuh do," said Jordan hypocritically. "I got tuh loose herd my cattle out on the flats till he shows up too."

Micky slid her hand from his clutching grasp and instinctively wiped it down the side of her riding skirt. Her face reflected her dismay and the intense thought that went with it as she tried to find a way out of this dilemma. Gene watched her closely, and liked what he saw.

So did Johnny Hines who had ridden up during

her conversation with Jordan. Gene looked casually at Johnny and immediately spotted Johnny's six-gun in its accustomed place. That explained Johnny's delay in getting to the stockyards. He had detoured to get it after the incident of the appaloosa bronc. Johnny's eyes were riveted on Micky Hardesty's flushed face. He looked exactly as though he had backed into a kicking mule.

Micky reached her decision, an over-generous decision. She looked at the marshal and her smile was very appealing. "I don't see how you could be blamed, Mr. Jordan," she said. "I just play in hard luck, I guess."

Jordan seemed relieved. "Mebbe yore hard luck's my good luck," he said. "I shorely would admire tuh take yuh tuh the hotel fer supper this evenin'."

Micky Hardesty warded off his clumsy gallantry with a practiced ease. "You're very kind, Mr. Jordan," she smiled sweetly, "but after we get the cattle bedded down on the flats out there, I'll have to help Boomer on night guard to keep them from getting mixed up with your brand. Perhaps after I sell my steers, you might repeat your invitation." She smiled again at Jordan.

Micky thought he was on her side. "If your men will let Boomer go," she said, "he and I will get started out with the steers. I'll give the station agent a due bill for the watering charge and pay it after I sell. Will that be satisfactory?"

The marshal looked over at the station agent and one eyelid drooped ever so slightly.

"Certainly not!" snapped the pompous little man. "Them charges is due in cash right now. Cash or some security. And I don't want no cattle offered me neither."

"There ain't nothin' I can do with him, Miss Hardesty," said Jordan in seeming sorrow. "He's within his rights when he says cash. Now I'd be proud tuh help yuh out but the truth is, I'm short of cash myself." He shook his head.

It came out so smoothly, so logically that Micky didn't suspect the master plan behind it. Her sudden inspiration had crumbled and she cast about wildly in her mind for a satisfactory solution to her problem.

Gene squeezed Champ with his knees. Champ shook himself all over and gave a piercing whinny that made Star Jordan jump and drop his hat in surprise.

Micky's face lighted up when she saw the team that had saved her from a similar predicament at the windmill down in the valley. She did not connect the two incidents as being parts of one great master plan.

"Oh Mr.—" she began.

Gene cut her off quickly by saying, "Dean, Miss. Buster Dean, at your service." He swept off his hat in the way she remembered from before.

Micky struggled to keep her amazement from showing in her face. The glad light went out of her eyes to be replaced by a sudden suspicion. *Why had he been so quick to give her another name? What did he have to hide?* Then she jumped to a girl-like conclusion. *But, of course, she had forgotten that Jordan was a law officer. She must not mention his helping her at the windmill.* Having jumped to this conclusion, Micky tried to cover up her error.

"Excuse me," she said hastily, "you looked like someone I used to know."

"I wish that I were," said Gene gallantly. "But perhaps I can get to know you better." His face brightened at the thought. "There's no time like the present," he added.

Micky hastily shook her head. If this man was avoiding the law, she couldn't involve him in her own troubles. She was casting around for something innocent to say when Star Jordan's heavy voice cut through her thoughts.

The marshal didn't like the way things were going. This dressed-up stranger hadn't been in his plan at all. He made a bold move to restore his importance to Miss Hardesty.

"Yuh there, stranger," he addressed Gene directly, "whatter yuh doin' with yore gun on? Don't yuh know it's agin the law in Hackberry? Shuck it, real pronto."

The short hairs on Gene's neck rose in pure

anger at this gross travesty of a law officer. His whole instinct cried out to him to goad the marshal into drawing and then gun him down to rid the earth of his kind forever. But he couldn't do it. The disciplined mind of the dedicated law man forced him to play the game as he had outlined it to Johnny back there in the pass.

He had seen just enough since he rode into Hackberry to know that he had been right. Star Jordan was just the symbol of evil. Somewhere behind him, moving the strings that made Jordan jump, was the brains of the Golden Ladder gang. Gene already had a well-founded suspicion whose brains those were. These thoughts raced through his mind in a flash but when he answered the marshal, his voice and his brain were under tight control.

"Why, Marshal," said Gene and the dangerous edge to his voice was lost on the unwitting Jordan, "I just purely haven't been in Hackberry yet. So, of course, I couldn't know about your law."

"Yuh know about it now," blustered Jordan. "I jes tol' yuh. Gimme thet fancy gun. Ain't thet a rifle too?"

"I can't do that," said Gene. "I just can't."

"Why not?" roared the marshal.

"I'm not in your town," was Gene's cool reply, "and until I am, I wear my guns. Man has a right to wear his guns on the trail. Might get robbed if he didn't. I'll just wear them until I unsaddle in your bailiwick. This horse and this saddle and these guns, why, Marshal, they're all I own. You wouldn't want me to get robbed of my sole possessions, would you now?"

Jordan saw a chance to make himself look good with Micky. "It's all right tuh wear 'em till yuh gits intuh town," he said. "I know trail law jest as well as the next man. But yuh shucks 'em pronto at the livery stable."

He turned to Micky with a smug look on his face that said, *I'm really a reasonable man just trying to do his duty.* His self-satisfaction was rudely shattered by Johnny Hines who kneed his bay horse forward a step or two.

"You shore are makin' it easy to rob that dressed-up pilgrim, ain't you, Jordan?" said Johnny Hines.

His movement and his voice carried up and into the stockyards where Pres and Cal perched on the crosswalk above the center loading chute. Pres shook his head sadly and spoke almost to himself.

"There goes Young Lochinvar like a locoed mule. Trouble and pretty girls are his weaknesses and when a pretty girl and trouble come hand and hand, that Johnny—" Again Pres shook his head.

Cal was so absorbed that he forgot to ask Pres what he meant. The knotted threads of plot and counter plot were unfolding before his very eyes and Cal was trying hard to watch them all and understand them.

Jordan wheeled in startled annoyance at Johnny's voice. "Yuh here again?" he asked, and his eyes flickered to the gun on Johnny's hip. "What'er yuh doin' with thet gun on? Yuh're still in town."

Johnny shook his head. "Nuh-unh," said Johnny. "I bought me a bottle of horse liniment and put on my gun. I was aimin' to go home and I sure ain't goin' without my equalizer here. Somebody might want to steal my house so's they'd have a place to put my stove."

"If yuh was headed home," said Jordan, "how come yuh're messin' around here?"

"Oh," said Johnny calmly, "thought I'd ride by and let you know I was goin' so's you could warn your men that if they come messin' around Spur Spring, they'd be fitting themselves for a long pine box."

"Yuh talk a lot, Hines," growled Star Jordan. "Git goin' 'fore I stop you permanent!"

"Me leave?" asked Johnny in simulated wonder. "Not on your tintype. This is my lucky day. I just miss gettin' planted by a cinch-cutting louse and then I rides this way to find Miss, Miss —" he paused hopefully.

"Hardesty," said the girl, hoping to prevent trouble, "Micaela Hardesty."

"My," said Johnny, "that's a pretty name." His voice held deep sincerity and his eyes were warm with appreciation.

"I like Micky better," said Gene and bowed in his saddle.

The girl blushed and Johnny took quick notice how it heightened her beauty.

"Yessireebobcat," said Johnny evenly, before Jordan could collect his thoughts, "it sure is my lucky day when I can find Miss Hardesty bein' flim-flammed by a crooked marshal with a dressed-up dude simperin' and smirkin' on the sidelines."

He looked at Jordan and he looked at Gene and there was a definite challenge in his eyes. Then Johnny looked directly at the girl.

"Miss Hardesty," he said, "you just bring your steers out to my place at Spur Spring. It ain't too far a drive, and they's plenty of water and plenty of feed. You use it and welcome just so's you won't think all men are no good."

The look of relief and thanks that flooded across Micky's face made Johnny's toes curl inside his boots. He was so intent on the girl that he didn't see the look of venomous disappointment on Jordan's face. *The Boxed H herd had to stay close to Hack-berry; that was the way it had been planned.*

Gene saw the look on Jordan's face, saw the stealthy movement of his gun arm toward the shoul-der hide-out. He had to stop that and he had to stop the Boxed H herd from moving out to Spur Spring. Jordan would have been trying to use his gun on Gene, not Johnny, if he had known Gene's reason

*Johnny Tipped His Hat to Micky*

for apparently siding with him.

Micky Hardesty looked squarely into Johnny's admiring eyes until she had to drop her glance. "I certainly appreciate your offer, Mr. —" she stopped in embarrassment and then laughed in her throaty voice. "Why I don't even know your name," she said in surprise.

"It's Hines, Miss Hardesty," said Johnny quickly, "but you can call me Johnny if you'd like to. It sounds better than Mr. Hines and you'll like it at Spur Spring." Johnny was bubbling over with eagerness.

Gene saw Jordan's arm slide under his vest and knew he had to move fast.

"I'm sure Miss Hardesty would like it at your ranch," said Gene and his tone was almost mocking. "But you see, it can't be done as easily as it sounds, my redheaded Sir Galahad."

Jordan stopped his stealthy draw with a look of puzzled pleasure on his face.

Johnny couldn't believe his ears. He forgot completely the part that Gene had to play and he forgot his own part in Gene's plan to bring the Golden Ladder gang to justice. Johnny had fallen head over chaps for Micky Hardesty and he stared at Gene with an angry face.

"Why can't it, you overdressed, prettied-up, four-flushing saddle tramp?" yelled Johnny. "You don't reckon you can stop it, do you?"

"I don't have to stop it," said Gene, with an outward calmness. "The marshal here will stop it, and he's got good reason to stop it. There's a little matter of watering charges that has to be settled. Of course," said Gene dryly, "if you have one hundred hard round dollars to pay the station agent, why I feel sure the marshal would be happy to release Miss Hardesty's cattle. Isn't that right, Marshal?"

Jordan's wolfish face split in a wide, fanged grin. "Shore is, stranger. I'd be right proud tuh put up the money myself fer Mis' Hardesty iffen I wasn't plum strapped for *dinero*."

Gene nodded briskly. "I'm sure you would, Marshal, and I know just how you feel," he said. "I'd be happy to put my own purse at her disposal if I had one."

Gene noticed Johnny's expression get even more determined and it gave him a sudden inspiration. "I'm just a penniless saddle tramp, according to Mr. Hines," he said, "and that doesn't give me much of a show to help a lady in distress. You're broke, Marshal, you say?"

Jordan hypocritically nodded his head.

"It just seems to me," said Gene smoothly, "that Mr. Hines being a man of property as he claims to be, ought to be able to bail Miss Hardesty out of her predicament. That is, if he's sincere and not making a windy play to show off."

"I'll show you two tinhorns," gritted Johnny.

"You, Jordan!" he barked, "you been tryin' to get your greedy paws on Spur Spring, ain't you? Well, here's your chance. Your word oughta be good with that triple distilled essence of polecat juice that masquerades as a station agent. You tell him to release Miss Hardesty's steers and I'll give you a deed to Spur Spring that you can hold in your grimy clutch until she sells her steers and can pay off the money."

Micky shook her head. "Thank you, Johnny," she said, "but the Boxed H fights its own battles." She gave Gene a scornful look. "I took help once on the way to Hackberry but I'll not do it again."

Johnny looked her full in the face and his monumental anger seemed to cool. "Miss Hardesty," said Johnny, "they's nothin' you can do about it now. I done made my play and if you don't side with it, why then I'll just naturally ride off and leave Spur Spring forever. Do you want me to do that?"

Micky saw what was in his heart shining out his eyes, and took refuge in silence.

Johnny turned to the marshal triumphantly. "Well, Star Jordan, how about it?" The fact that he ignored Gene completely showed how confident he felt.

Jordan tried hard to mask his eagerness but his voice betrayed him. "That shore oughta be all right with you," he said to the station agent. "My word's good for the money, ain't it?"

Gene detected a note of menace in the marshal's

closing words to the agent.

The station agent seemed to be listening with only half an ear, if that. The tobacco can sounder on the telegraph key in the station was chattering. The sound came across the clear desert air like a piece of tin held against a rapidly spinning bicycle wheel.

"Eh, Marshal, what's that?" he asked. "Oh, you want to stand good for the watering charge. Sure, sure, that's fine with me. Anything you say. Fix it up, I gotta go. That's my signal—regular afternoon schedule." He scuttled off toward the station as fast as his short legs could carry him.

Gene listened to the chattering telegraph and his practiced ear automatically translated the code into words. The operator at Barstow was clearing his hook on the east-bound schedule and he was really pounding brass. The train orders and the station instructions were a rolling rataplan of railroad routine that Gene deciphered almost unconsciously until a succession of words strung together in his mind and made him start.

#9 SPCL EB MAIL ON TIME EX BARTW ONE EXP CHST BNKNTS MKD MDSE CONSGD BNK HKBRY CNSNEE MST TK DLVY DIRECT DRNG WTR STP CONFIRM.

The sounder went quiet as the Hackberry agent opened his circuit to reply.

Johnny was oblivious to everything but the fact that he had made his point good. "You heard the agent, Jordan," he stormed. "Open them gates and get your men outta the way so we can get started."

Jordan was about to comply with Johnny's request since he had Hines's word before witnesses about Spur Spring, when Gene again intervened.

"It seems to me," said Gene without a flicker of expression on his handsome face, "that some sort of legal document should be drawn up just so's everybody's protected." He had to get those Boxed H steers out of the corrals, and onto the flats without letting Johnny take them to Spur Spring.

"What are you buttin' in for?" yelled the exasperated Johnny. "I told you once before this afternoon not to mess with me and my problems. Now, by Godfrey, I'll give you somethin' to make you remember it."

He started to ride toward Gene with fire in his eye when Micky stopped him.

"I would feel better about it, Johnny," she said, "if there were a legal deed drawn up. I would not have thought it necessary where men are concerned, not real men, that is; but if it's down in writing, there can be no possible misunderstanding." She managed to convey the impression that she was talking about Gene.

"Micaela," began Gene, when she interrupted.

"Miss Hardesty to you," she said icily.

"Miss Hardesty is quite right," said Gene, ignoring the interruption. "It should be done in legal style and put in writing."

Star Jordan didn't know who this fancy stranger was or where he came from but he was playing Jordan's game.

"Thet makes sense tuh me," said Jordan. "I'll hustle one of the boys after lawyer Gosslen. He'll know how tuh fix it up."

*Yes,* thought Gene to himself, *I imagine he will.* He looked down at the marshal and smiled. "You're in luck," Gene said out loud, "I guess that's Mr. Gosslen now standing over there by the station platform."

The marshal craned his neck and let out a satisfied grunt.

"Yep, thet's him," he said, and let out a bellow that Gosslen acknowledged by an airy wave of his cane as he started slowly toward them. "Shore lucky he was a' standin' there," said Jordan to no one in particular. "We'd have tuh ride down tuh his house, gen'lly."

Gene nodded while his mind raced over certain possibilities. Could Gosslen have been standing there for some reason besides just chance? The station agent said the telegraph chatter was the regular afternoon schedule of orders and instructions. Was Gosslen listening to those orders? If he was listening, why? And could he read the railroad code? And why had the station agent stopped in his rush for the station to talk with Gosslen, almost as if he were reporting to his boss for instructions?

There were a lot of questions in Gene's mind that needed answering right quick and Johnny, drat him, was girl-struck.

Mr. J. Francis Gosslen was all suavity as he listened to the marshal's explanation. He nodded sympathetically toward Miss Hardesty as if deploring the silly railroad regulations that had involved her so unpleasantly. When the marshal told him of Johnny Hines's offer, Mr. Gosslen seemed moved to salute such a generous spirit with a flourish of his cane.

When the marshal concluded his speech by saying, "Yes, sir, thet Hines was achin' to get goin' when this stranger said we oughta have it done legal," Mr. Gosslen looked at Gene and there was the suspicion of a sardonic grin at the corners of his mouth.

"What about it, Gosslen?" Johnny said impatiently. "Get the papers ready and I'll sign 'em. We got to be movin'. It's a drive to Spur Spring and it's gettin' late."

"I appreciate the ardor of your desire, Mr. Hines," said Gosslen. "Unfortunately, legal matters do not always permit of youthful haste. I will prepare the papers this evening. You can sign them at my office after supper. Until then, I suggest that Miss Hardesty's steers remain in the stockyards for safekeeping."

Micky's face was a study in pure disappointment.

Johnny just looked disgusted.

"That means we'll have to hold 'em on the flats all night," said Johnny, "and with a big Ladder herd close enough to make me suspicious."

The marshal shrugged his shoulders, ignoring Johnny's barbed remark.

Only Gene seemed capable of stirring the matter up a little longer. "Mr. Gosslen," said Gene, "have you ever seen a little bunch of steers in a big railroad corral get spooked by passing trains?"

The somberly dressed man looked surprised. "Why no, Mr. Dean," he said. "I cannot say that I have."

"I have," said Gene. *He knows my go-by name already,* thought Gene. "They go crazy," he said aloud. "A train comes by with those steers in there all alone and they'll kill or cripple themselves something awful. Miss Hardesty will have a claim against the people that kept them there." This was one way to find out if Gosslen knew anything about #9EB, a special train.

"That is extremely sound reasoning," said J. Francis Gosslen. *Why did this stranger also want that herd out of the corrals?* "What do you suggest?"

Gene prayed that Johnny would wake up and catch the message he was trying to pass him with his voice. "Turn the steers out," said Gene crisply. "Let Miss Hardesty and her man Banning night-herd them on the flats away from the right of way. Put a couple of the marshal's deputies to guard them. To-morrow, after the papers have been signed, they can accept Mr. Hines's generous hospitality."

"Is that agreeable to you, Marshal Jordan?" asked the lawyer.

"Shore," said Jordan, "but I ain't got no regular deppitys. Only swear in the boys when there's somethin' special."

"Like rolling a drunk, or stealing a stove," said Johnny contemptuously. "I'll help Miss Micky." He used the name reverently. "I'll help her bed them steers down and hold them on night guard. Which is more'n I hear anyone else offerin' to do." He glared at Gene as he spoke and Gene knew that Johnny really was far gone. "Yessireebobcat," said Johnny, "you can even deputize me, Jordan, and I won't ask no pay for it."

"Deppitize yuh?" snorted Jordan. "Yuh think I'm plum *locoed?*"

"I would hate to ask that question of an intelligent jury," said Gosslen bitingly. "I think Mr. Hines's offer is very fair. I recommend that you follow it, Marshal Jordan." Gene noticed that he accented the word "recommend."

Jordan looked at Johnny; then he looked at Gosslen. He turned to Johnny unwillingly.

"Yuh're a Deppity without pay," he said.

Then he turned to his henchmen who were still holding Banning and guarding the stockyard gate.

"Les go, boys," he growled. "And give thet old rana-han back his rifle. He might want tuh shoot hisself fer bein' suh ornery."

Boomer Banning shook his arms to start the circulation flowing and grabbed his rifle from the Ladder man who had been holding it. With quick, deft movements, the grizzled old puncher stuffed it with shells. When it was fully loaded, he levered a shell into the breech and eased the hammer down on the loaded chamber.

"Now, you varmints," croaked Boomer, addressing the nonplussed Ladder men, Jordan, Gosslen and Gene Autry, "hits loaded fer the fust time since we came into this here valley. Thet's fair warnin'." He stumped over to his horse, swung into the saddle and opened the stockyards gate in a swooping movement.

Johnny and Micky rode inside to move the steers out while Banning rode off from the gate to check them when they came out a'snufflin'.

Gene kneed Champ off to one side of the great plank gate, where he dismounted to check his latigo knot.

J. Francis Gosslen denoted his presence by a delicate clearing of his throat.

"You are a very intelligent man," said Gosslen, "very intelligent Mr. — Mr. —"

"Dean, Buster Dean," supplied Gene. *Gosslen had used this name before. Why did he seem to falter and forget it now?*

"Of course," said the lawyer. "How careless of me to forget." He smiled deprecatingly. "As I was about to say, this is the second time this afternoon that you have interfered with my plans. Perhaps it would be better if—" he seemed to hesitate on his next word ever so slightly.

"If what?" asked Gene in simulated curiosity.

"If we tried working together," said Gosslen smoothly.

Gene seemed to consider this proposal and found it attractive. "Just give it a name, Mr. Gosslen," he said.

Gosslen looked around cautiously and folded his hands over the head of his cane. "It would be better if we discussed the matter privately," he said. "I will send word when and where."

Gene nodded and Gosslen seemed satisfied with the way his approach had been received. "Once again, Mr. Dean," said Gosslen, "let me congratulate you on using your head before your hands."

Out of the tail of his eye, Gene noticed that the Boxed H steers had cleared the gate. Now, Johnny and Micky rode through the gate behind them. Gene waited until they came abreast of him. Then he spoke to Gosslen in a voice loud enough for Johnny to hear. "It's not easy to use your head, Mr. Gosslen," he said, "when any ordinary fool can use his hands or his feet."

Johnny's reaction was all that Gene had hoped.
He wheeled the blaze-faced bay horse on his hind
feet and literally tumbled from his saddle to rush at
Gene in a blind fury. Gosslen sidled to one side and
watched the fight with a smirk of satisfaction on his
face.

Gene waited until Johnny's headlong charge was
almost on top of him. His right hand shot forward
and grasped Johnny's extended left. Using Johnny's
momentum, he snapped him toward himself and his
right hip became a lever that bumped Johnny's feet
out from under him with a powerful thrust. Gene
broke his own grip on Johnny's arm and the redhead went sailing through the air to sprawl in the
dust and roll against the stockyard fence with a re-
sounding smack.

Gene pivoted on his heel and lit on top of Johnny.
He grasped Johnny by both shoulders and banged
his head up and down in the dirt. "Don't be a fool,"
said Gene in low intense tones. "We're playing for
high stakes. Johnny, you idiot, do you hear what I'm
saying?"

Gene's familiar voice sliced into the fog of love
and battle that clouded Johnny's eyes. Gene almost
hoped he had beaten his message into Johnny's head
when a whirlwind of feminine fury hit him across
the shoulders with her quirt.

"You—you—you—" sputtered Micky, "you four-
flushing dude!" The quirt kept up its stinging tat-

too; Micky was too mad to make it cut.

Gene was laughing so hard inside he could scarcely collect himself to jump free of the twisting Johnny who had taken quick advantage of the interruption to give a demonstration of a bucking horse. Gene sprang clear and as he did, Johnny caught one flying foot and twisted it. Gene lit on the back of his neck, like a well-trained acrobat and rolled over and onto his feet. He whirled to see and hear Johnny groan loudly and lift his arms toward Micky Hardesty.

"Oh Mr. Hines, Johnny, Johnny," sobbed the overwrought girl.

"Say it again," said that unabashed young man, "it sure sounds pretty."

Gene was already in his saddle when J. Francis Gosslen walked over to him. "Women have no appreciation of brains," sighed the lawyer. "All they understand is the silly emotion produced by animal strength." He smiled knowingly up at Gene. "You and I, Mr. Dean, use our brains," said Gosslen. "I will let you know when we can put them to our mutual profit."

He twirled his cane idly as he turned away toward Hackberry.

Champ felt the guiding pressure of Gene's knee and wheeled toward the livery stable. As he turned, Gene saw Micky Hardesty helping an ostentatiously limping Johnny toward his horse.

Gene smiled wryly. *It looks like the Strawberry Roan has met his match,* he thought to himself as he rode away.

His face became a mask of intense thought as he fitted the afternoon's events into their proper pattern. He knew the rungs in the Golden Ladder gang now, knew them clear to the top. All that he had to do was to climb them, and he'd have to climb them alone if Johnny didn't snap out of it.

# CHAPTER SIX

## AN EXCITING MEAL

Pres jumped down off the crosswalk and headed toward the livery stable in long and hurried strides, a gait that matched his thoughts, when Cal caught up with him.

"Pres," said Cal, "there are so many things I don't understand like why did—" But his questions were stopped before they even started.

Pres halted in his tracks and shook his head reprovingly.

"Cal," he said seriously, "don't you get started with whys, what-fors and how-comes. Not now, nohow. There's too many marked cards in this deck that your Uncle Pres don't understand."

"What?" asked Cal.

"What!" ejaculated Pres. "Well, now you listen with both ears. *Savvy?*"

Cal nodded.

"For one thing," said Pres, "there's the funny fact that Pretty Shadow and Star Jordan both seem to want them Boxed H steers to spend the night out on the flats where they'll be right handy to the Ladder herd that Jordan's aholdin' out there. That don't add up—and don't ask me why," Pres added as he saw Cal's mouth open.

Cal closed it.

"For another thing," said Pres ticking it off on his fingers, "Johnny Hines doesn't like the idea of holding the Boxed H and their pretty boss near the Ladders either. Yet, when he puts his head down like a bull at a gate and starts to scrimmage with Pretty Shadow, he lives to get helped away by that aforesaid Boxed H boss. He had every chance in the world of getting himself killed if the handsome-dressed stranger had a'wished it thataway. Course it could be that Johnny was just lucky or appealed to a tender spot in Mr. Whatever-He-Calls-Himself Dean's heart, or that they done it a'purpose. Shuckins, I've seen two squaws bust one another worse. Finally, there's old buzzard face."

"You mean Gosslen?" asked Cal quickly.

"Don't you interrupt me when I'm thinking real good," said Pres with mock severity. "Old buzzard face shines up to Pretty Shadow and the two of them look likes they're going to be as thick as flies in a syrup jug. Nossir, your self-appointed uncle, Pres Wesley, Esquire, has to go off by himself in the dark of the moon and do a big think about these here random fragments of idle thought."

"What about Miss Hardesty?" said Cal.

Pres looked at him with an exasperated frown. "Oh no you don't, Calico Cat," said Pres. "The one thing I don't aim to add to my mental hazards is tryin' to figure out what that girl has on her mind. You just remember, Cal, that you can lose your mind in easier ways than tryin' to figure what a woman has in her think tank."

"How?" said Cal eagerly.

"Well," said Pres, "for one thing, you can try playing a crooked roulette wheel. It's quicker and less painful. Now, let's go and wash up for supper."

They were swinging in to the back corral of the livery stable when Hermie Gerbode drove slowly out in a light spring wagon drawn by two sleek and placid mares.

"Hi, Hermie," called Pres. "You takin' a drive in the cool of the evening for your health?"

"Ach, Bres," was Hermie's quiet reply, "I am bast such foolishmendts. Der iss a chipmendt by exbress I musdt bick up so soon der train komms yet. A spechall order." He smiled with a secret pleasure and drove off behind his fat and ambling team.

Pres produced soap and a reasonably clean towel from the jockey box of his freight wagon and Cal and he soused their heads and arms in the icy water of the mammoth trough. Cal came up sputtering and groped for the towel. When his eyes were cleared of the water that streamed down from his plastered hair, they fastened on Gene Autry who had ridden in to the livery stable.

Gene was hanging his saddle, bridle, martingale,

and saddle blankets carefully on the pegs provided for that purpose but seldom used by careless cowboys eager for the delights of town. Most riders used the feed troughs in the stable stalls, troughs possibly infected with diseases of the range. Gene took an empty grain sack and with his razor sharp knife, slit it up each side from the middle, about three inches in from the seam leaving a deep pocket of sack with a flap hanging down on either side. The two straps were tied together forming a crude but effective nosebag.

Gene put a generous feed of cracked corn in the morral and slid the headstrap gently over Champ's ears, and scratched them affectionately as the great horse nuzzled him through the coarse burlap before he began to eat. Gene then took a bucket of sun-warmed water and carefully washed Champ's back while the great horse tossed his head to get the last bits of grain out of the morral.

"It don't make sense," said Pres, and Cal hurriedly began to dry his face.

"What doesn't make sense, Pres?" he said between swipes at his hair with a comb he found in his pocket.

"Cal, no man who takes care of his horse that way," Pres nodded toward Gene, "has any truck with the likes of J. Francis Gosslen unless he's got some powerful good reason behind it." Pres's face contorted in thought and smoothed out again. "I allus did think better on a full stomach," said Pres.

"Come on, Calico Cat, before it's all gone."

Hermie Gerbode's eating house, sandwiched between the store and the hotel under the same massive roof, had a reputation for good feeding. The men of the Hualapai Valley, and the infrequent women who could stand the strain of desert living, thought of Hackberry as the place where Gerbode set a good table. The townspeople of Hackberry, married and single, ate there whenever they could figure out a good excuse for themselves.

The long dining-room was crowded when Pres and Cal stepped through the door that led from the general store, and Pres automatically stopped a moment just to feast his eyes and whet his appetite.

J. Francis Gosslen was seated at his accustomed table in the far corner of the room. Pres noted this with an eye trained to look for fixtures in their usual position. His eyes roamed about the dining-room, just to see if anything had changed while he had been absent on his last freight trip. It all looked the same but there was one glaring and conspicuous difference that made Pres blink when he saw it.

Johnny Hines, as clean as soap and water vigorously applied could make him, sat at a table right spang in the center of the room. Micky Hardesty sat beside him. Her honey-colored hair curled down in a graceful waving cloak to the level of her shoulders and one ear peeked demurely through the soft strands of hair.

*Pres and Cal Stepped into the Dining-Room*

She had changed her work shirt for a blouse of plum-colored silk that was gathered around her slim waist with a turquoise-studded belt and her riding skirt was the whitest hand-tanned buckskin. A tiny pulse beat danced up and down in the hollow of her throat that was exposed by the low rounded collar of her blouse. She was all rounded curves and soft femininity to the untrained eye, but an underlying hint of iron determination was there for all her youthful beauty.

If Johnny Hines knew this facet of her character, he gave no indication of it in his manner. His usual loquacity, his hearty boisterous greetings for his proven friends was missing. He was so intent on the girl beside him that he ignored completely Pres and Cal as they passed his table on their way to the one Pres had selected.

The only windows in the dining-room were at the front where a door opened inward between them from the platform porch. Pres seated himself at one of these tables, tucked his napkin under his chin and regarded Cal with a quizzical stare.

"I always did like to pick a seat where I could make my own exit in a hurry," said Pres, nodding toward the window beside them.

The meaning of his remark was lost on Cal who could not take his eyes off the table. A tin knife and fork and spoon, clean but battered, flanked a plate of extraordinary size and thickness, a little chipped around the edges. A huge china mug, as thick as the plate and equally well worn bespoke a Territory's love of coffee, as black as ink, as sweet as honey, and as hot as Hackberry.

A reasonable imitation of a longhorn steer was glazed into the chinaware. Hermie Gerbode had sent all the way to his native land for this one touch of elegance. The red-checked tablecloth was held down by huge bowls of sliced raw purple onions, stewed canned tomatoes, heavy with sugar, pinto beans with generous slices of lean ham floating among them, mashed potatoes, and an even larger bowl of canned green-gage plums for dessert. A pitcher of coffee steamed fitfully among the bowls while a smaller pitcher proved to be full of thick brown-flour gravy. All these vessels surrounded an island of condiments formed by salt and pepper shakers and a shallow dish of red chili peppers swimming in vinegar.

To top it off, a plump motherly-looking woman came by their table. Her left arm was lined with platters from palm to elbow, and one of these deftly transferred itself from her arm to the table. It was heaped high with steaks pan-broiled in their own tallow.

"Eat up, Cal," said Pres loading his own plate. "Hermie charges just as much if you go easy on the grub. Hermie says he cooks it to be eaten."

Cal didn't know quite where to start, but he had filled his plate to the very rim when a sibilant hiss from Pres made him look toward the hotel side of the dining-room.

Gene made an eye-filling picture as he stood in the door that entered the dining-room from the hotel lobby. His eyes seemed to sweep across the crowded dining-room. They were the eyes of a desert hawk who scans the earth below and never misses a thing but who is always a part of the clean, high air of the far places of the west. The clean-cut strength and the pulsing vitality of his athletic body were magnified, not hidden by his clothes.

A silk neckerchief was knotted around his throat above a checked shirt of softest wool. Tailored doeskin trousers that were rugged enough for hard riding but looked fit for a king were stuffed carefully into the tops of hand-tooled, bench-made boots that fit like gloves and were just as soft. A broad cartridge belt of finely carved leather, studded with gleaming brass cartridges, crisscrossed below the silver buckle of his belt. A long-barreled, perfectly balanced revolver rested snugly against his hip in a special holster that Gene had designed himself. A snow-white Stetson, broad-brimmed and creased down the crown, sat rakishly on top of an unruly thatch of sandy hair. Cal forgot to eat.

Gene finished his inspection of the dining-room and with his first step, he swept off his hat with a grace that showed an innate courtesy and good manners. He walked firmly into the room and turned to-

ward the door that opened onto the street. Johnny
and Micky gave no sign that they recognized him as
he passed their table. Johnny was still unconscious
of everything but the girl and the girl looked Gene
squarely in the face and cut him dead with a disdainful glance.

Gene chose the unoccupied table by the other
window, across the door from Pres and Cal, where he
could watch the dining-room and keep an eye on
Champ at the hitching rail outside. Cal's back was in
his own way and he turned his attention to his
heaped-up plate almost regretfully.

Cal had eaten his way down until he could see
china beneath his knife and fork when the door from
the porch flew open from a violent push. Star Jordan
stepped into the dining-room. His deadliest gunman,
Boy Nolan, stepped catfootedly behind him with a
baleful look on his saturnine face. Every eye in the
room was riveted on Jordan and his henchman as
they made their dramatic entrance. Every eye, that
is, except the four that belonged to Johnny Hines
and Micky Hardesty.

Johnny was looking at Micky with a dazed expression and his right hand was vigorously wielding
the salt shaker above his cup of coffee.

Jordan's heavy face reflected his rage at finding
Micky having supper with Johnny Hines. He walked
heavily toward them with each ponderous step jig-
gling the heavy china on the tables as he passed.

Nolan followed right behind him. A funereal hush fell over the crowded room and the air was heavy with menace.

Pres felt the nerve ends along his backbone tingle and he slewed his chair around until his legs and lap were clear of the table edge. If he had to move, it would have to be fast. He stole a quick glance past the still-open door at Gene and saw that he too, had freed himself for instant action. But Pres missed what Gene's trained eye saw—a hint of annoyance that flickered over the face of J. Francis Gosslen like heat lightning on a dry summer night.

Johnny was in the act of raising his self-salted coffee to his lips when Jordan deliberately slapped his elbow with a hamlike hand. The hot liquid cascaded over the rim of the cup. The cup dropped from Johnny's instinctive backward jerk and Micky gave a little piercing scream as the coffee bit through her skirt. Jordan grinned thinly and was already a step beyond the scene of his deliberate discourtesy when one of Johnny's legs uncoiled from beneath the table to lash out and sweep Jordan's feet from under him.

Nolan took a quick angling step to dodge Johnny's backward flying chair and Jordan scrambled to his feet with an oath to face a thoroughly angry Johnny.

"Yuh're a deppity marshul," gritted Jordan, "why ain't yuh out watchin' them steers stid of watchin' their boss?"

Micky's hand tugged at Johnny's sleeve in a plea

for caution. "We came in to eat," said Johnny, with ill-concealed rage. "When we get through, we'll go back and let Banning come in. You got any objections, Marshal?" The title was an epithet as Johnny said it.

"Yuh git back tuh yore job," said Jordan. "I'll see thet Mis' Hardesty gits taken care of. An' be shore yuh're wearin' a gun nex' time I see yuh. I'm warnin' yuh." Jordan seemed to relish taunting Johnny when he saw Nolan's position. Johnny was caught between two fires if he made a move.

"I'll go back to being a deputy marshal when Miss Micky's ready," said Johnny flatly. "And not before. As for wearing a gun, Jordan, I hung mine on my saddle when we came inside. I never did figure that being a law officer gave me license to do what other folks couldn't. But you can bet your last stolen dollar that I'll be wearing a gun the next time we meet."

"Thet kind of talk is plenty cheap," sneered Jordan.

"Mebbe it is," said Johnny, "but if you think it's so cheap, then you listen to this." His voice reached every corner of the room. "A man ought to wear a gun day and night in Hackberry or out of it," cried Johnny. "You think you're smart enough to shoot a skunk at three paces and still dodge the stink, Jordan, but it sticks to you. It's the carrion stink of a corpse-eating polecat that burns houses, steals cattle, kicks women and children out of their own homes, and poisons waterholes. A man has a duty to carry a gun when the face of the land is cluttered up with the likes of you."

Johnny stopped for a second and then his voice came slow and evenly spaced. "You hide behind a lawman's star, Jordan, because you ain't got the nerve to be crooked openly and you ain't got the character to be honest. You're nothin' but a sheepherder turned cinch cutter."

Gene tensed in his chair. Johnny had opened his mouth too wide and said too much.

"Iffen yuh say I cut thet cinch, yore a liar," howled Jordan.

Splatt! Johnny's open hand, stiff-armed with the full pivot force of his wiry body behind it took Jordan on the side of the face. The big man staggered off balance with an anguished roar.

Nolan's arm whipped down to his low slung gun and several things happened simultaneously.

Twin streaks of masculine fury catapulted from each side of the front door.

Gene hurled his whole trained body into a perfect football tackle that took Johnny around the knees and stretched him on the floor out of danger.

Pres Wesley didn't bother with tackling Nolan. The force of his charge swept Nolan into his arms and with an upward sweep, Pres hurled the gunman full tilt down the dining-room while his drawn gun exploded harmlessly into the ceiling and was lost when he hit the floor.

Johnny dragged the tablecloth with him as he went down. Gene's quick eye and quicker hand spotted what he wanted among the wreckage and a thick red stream trickled down Johnny's forehead from his scalp. He lay still beneath Gene's protecting body.

Cal was standing on his chair trying to follow both plays when he saw Jordan regain his balance and draw his shoulder gun at the same time. Gene and Johnny were so mixed up on the floor with the tablecloth that Jordan had trouble getting the bead he wanted. Cal grabbed his heavy, unused coffee cup and let it go with all his force and a prayer. His aim was good and his prayer was answered. The cup took Jordan behind the left ear with a noise like beef being cut on a butcher's block. Jordan shook his head once and slowly toppled over onto the floor.

Micky was looking wildly for something heavy to use on Gene when the icy voice of J. Francis Gosslen spoke almost in her ear.

"Control yourself, young lady," he said. "I am certain that Mr. Dean was not so hasty as to damage your protector permanently."

As if fitting his actions to these words, Gene helped Johnny to his feet. Micky burst out sobbing when she saw him.

Johnny explored his head with tentative fingers and withdrew them to gaze curiously at the sticky red substance that covered them. He put one finger in his mouth in an unconscious gesture and a surprised look made his face look like the old Johnny Hines again.

Then Gene's voice completed the transformation. "You're a deputy marshal," said Gene, "and it's my bounden duty to escort you back to your post."

"What if I won't go?" said Johnny with an impish tone to his voice.

Gene's silver-mounted gun flashed into Johnny's stomach, while Micky stifled her sobs in sudden amazement.

"You'll go," said Gene, "or I'll shoot you and drag your body out there. You make it easy on yourself."

"I'll go," said Johnny hastily and J. Francis Gosslen chimed in.

"As long as you are taking him out of danger for his own good, Mr. Dean," said Gosslen, "would you mind bringing him to my office and letting him sign the proper papers regarding Spur Spring before something unfortunate occurs to make it impossible?"

Gene looked around the room before he answered. Jordan was still prone and motionless on the floor. Nolan crawled dazedly between the tables looking for his gun. Gene looked at Gosslen and shook his head.

"I'm taking him out of town without stopping," he said. "This bird belongs to me, Mr. Gosslen.

*"You'll Go," Said Gene, "Or I'll Shoot You—"*

Nobody else gets a crack at him until I've had my turn."

Gosslen's face mirrored his disgust at men who let a woman make such fools of them. Gene saw this expression and it suited him just fine.

"Get along you," said Gene prodding Johnny with his gun muzzle, and the little procession marched from the dining-room, Johnny and Micky in front, and Gene walking steadily behind.

Johnny seemed to have his whole attention devoted to reassuring Micky but as they passed a table, Johnny's hand swept out and plucked a napkin from it which he clapped to his forehead.

Pres and Cal stood on the porch and watched the three-horse cavalcade ride out of town in the same order that they had left the dining-room. Pres sighed contentedly and patted his stomach as he selected one of the comfortable rawhide-bottomed chairs that lined the porch and tilted himself back against the wall.

"Those green-gages surelee hit the spot," said Pres.

Cal's voice was angry and full of protest. "How can you watch Mr. Hines riding out there to get killed?" stormed Cal.

Pres looked at him from under his hat brim. "Calico Cat," said Pres slowly, "Johnny Hines may get killed someday but it won't never happen so long as that fellow that uses Dean for his go-by name is around. You're a right handy fellow with a china mug, Cal," said Pres reflectively, "but you just don't savvy the burro."

"What burro?" asked Cal perplexedly.

Pres sighed. "That's just a handle for a situation," he said. "Whenever a man gets so's he can out-think one of them desert mockingbirds, he's got a right to call himself a prospector."

"I see," said Cal, who didn't.

"I don't think you do," said Pres agreeably. "If you did, you wouldn't be disturbing my digestion with questions. You done seen Pretty Shadow snatch the red-tempered Hines out of two or maybe three jackpots today already and you still figger they're ring-tailed enemies."

Cal nodded. "That Mr. Dean is just trying to ingratiate himself with the marshal," he said.

"You use some real fancy words, Calico Cat," said Pres, "but I don't reckon you got any more brains than Star Jordan. That's a real disappointment to me. If you think Pretty Shadow is trying to butter himself with Jordan, that's just what he wants you, Jordan, me, Gosslen, and all Hackberry in general to think. Nunh-unh," said Pres firmly, "that ain't the way she lays."

"Then why did he help the marshal get the best of Johnny right in the dining-room?" asked Cal triumphantly.

"Calico Cat Calvin Ellicott," said Pres severely, "why did you throw that coffee mug at the marshal?"

Cal looked embarrassed. "It was the only thing I could think of," he said. "I thought you might get shot, Pres."

Pres stuck out his hand and they shook hands solemnly. "Thanks, pardner," said Pres, "now you know why Pretty Shadow, alias Buster Dean, alias his real name whatever it is, collared Johnny Hines."

"Why?" said Cal.

"Because, you sublime pilgrim," said Pres, "he was afraid Johnny Hines would get hurt. Me now," Pres went on, "I prides myself on thinking pretty rapid but that dressy dude beat me to it. You want to ask questions, Calico, or shall I dispense free information and give your tongue a rest?"

Cal nodded and said nothing.

"Me, I dived for that Nolan hombre," said Pres, "figuring him to be the danger. I aimed to let Jordan have my attentions later. Pretty Shadow now, he sized it up better'n me. There were Jordan and Nolan for sure against Hines. If I wasn't agin Hines, maybe I'd miss Nolan. He just knocked Hines down and then covered him with his own body. That's quick thinking and plenty nerve, Calico Cat. Me, myself," said Pres, "I aim to shake that dude by the hand next time we meet and just follow him around to learn how to act."

Cal's struggle to fit Pres's opinion into his own ideas was solved by Hermie Gerbode. His light spring wagon came out of the gathering dusk to stop alongside the platform in front of the store.

"Yo, Bres," called Hermie, "to me a handt giff mit dis gases."

Pres tilted his chair forward onto the porch and stepped over into the wagon bed with a mock grumble. The two men heaved the case onto the platform and then slid it inside the store. Pres looked down at the black lettering on the case—DRY GOODS— USE NO HOOKS.

"That's the heaviest dry goods I ever handled, Hermie," he said. "What is it, lead sheets for coffin linings?"

Hermie Gerbode mopped his brow with a quick swipe of his sleeve, and made sure that no one could overhear him before he replied.

"Bres," he said proudly, "it iss der baber money for der pank yet. Vee opens tomorrow und den, Hackberry hass a blace to komm for help that is honest yet."

Pres looked fondly at the roly-poly figure of Hermie Gerbode. "I'll be your best customer, Hermie," he promised. "I never can keep myself in spending money. Let's put it away so's it'll be here when I come to float a loan." Pres gestured toward the bricked-up corner of the store that was the bank.

"Nein," said Hermie, "dot iss nodt necessary. No vun knows ven it komms yet, und it iss safer right here in der pox so blainly markit DRY GOOTS. I put it avay tomorrow morning ven der store opens."

Pres nodded in agreement with Hermie's reasoning. No one would suspect one more box on the littered floor of Gerbode's General Store. He patted Hermie affectionately on the shoulder and stepped back on the porch.

Cal and Pres stood on the porch in silent companionship while dusk turned into deep purple, then into a soft and velvet black. The night wind came breathing down from the east and seemed to brush the sky with stardust as it passed. Borne on the wings of the wind, came the mournful whistle of the special transcontinental mail train, number nine eastbound, as it labored up the grade behind two engines. The whistles seemed relieved that the box of dry goods was now in Hackberry.

# CHAPTER SEVEN

## DECOY BY NIGHT

The sound of number nine's far-off and mournful whistle reached Gene's ears when he was half-way out to the flats where the Boxed H herd was bedded down. It was the only sound except the steady hoof-beats of the horses and the soft creaking of saddle leather that had broken the silence of their journey. Micky and Johnny rode in front and Gene had made no effort to break their apparent conspiracy of silence. Now he kneed Champ forward in a faster gait and came up directly behind Johnny and Micky until Champ's head was almost between their stirrups.

"I guess we're far enough from town," said Gene "so no prying eyes will see or hear what happens."

Johnny's hand shot across to grasp Micky's with a great tenderness when he heard the murmur of a six-gun against leather as Gene slid his Peacemaker into its holster.

"How's your head, Johnny?" asked Gene casually. "Bloody but still tough as ever?"

Johnny's voice was infectious. "I don't hold no hard feelin's for you a'tappin' me with that catsup bottle," he laughed, "but did you have to rub it in my hair? Darn stuff'll be there for days the way it's a'dryin' like cement."

Micky couldn't believe her ears and she didn't try. Womanlike, she reined her horse to an abrupt stop and spoke her mind.

"I won't go a step farther until I know what kind of a game you two are playing," she said petulantly. "I'm tired of all this excitement and suspense. Now you talk turkey, Johnny Hines."

Johnny was laughing so hard that he couldn't get his breath. Micky began tapping her quirt against her riding skirt and Gene recognized the sign.

"Johnny," he said, "you speak up before we both get into trouble."

Johnny caught his breath with a gasp and reached out to grab both of Micky's hands in his. "Miss Hardesty," said Johnny gravely, "I'd admire for you to meet my partner, Gene Autry."

"Is that his real name?" asked Micky suspiciously. "He's given me a couple of handles already today."

"Where'd you meet him?" asked Johnny.

"You better tell him, Miss Micky," said Gene. "He wouldn't believe me on a bet after that catsup bottle."

So Micky told Johnny about the stampede and the windmill and meeting Gene.

Then Johnny told Micky how he'd sent Gene a letter and why they had agreed to meet in Hackberry and not recognize one another until Gene gave the signal at the right moment.

"Yes," said Gene, "and when you came along, Johnny took one good look at you and forgot all about me. He threw himself into being the jealous young man until he had me worried. I was trying to keep him from getting killed prematurely and he was trying to massacre me every time I so much as looked in your direction. Miss Micky," said Gene earnestly, "you make more trouble than the Ladder gang. Why don't you stop it and settle down?"

The half-filled new moon didn't give enough light to reveal the delicate flush that crept over Micky's face. Johnny's voice cut in hastily to prevent embarrassing questions.

"How do you have it figgered, Gene?" he asked. "I mean the Ladders, not Miss Micky settlin' down."

"Well," said Gene easily, "one part of it looks open and shut. Miss Micky runs the Boxed H, and Jordan runs the Ladder. It doesn't take much savvy to see how a few strokes with a hot iron could transfer ownership from Miss Micky to Jordan. Just lengthen the two side lines and you have a Boxed H brand changed to the Ladder."

"I can't believe it," gasped Micky. "Jordan was the one who told me to drive my steers to Hackberry."

"Sure he did," said Gene. "If you drive them to Hackberry, he doesn't have to ride down to your range and steal them himself. Saves him time, money, and saddle sores. The windmill incident was to make sure they'd be good and thirsty when you got them here. They weren't but you watered them anyhow. The station agent trumps up a fake watering charge and you're in a jackpot with no money."

"But I still—" began Micky, and stopped as Gene went right ahead beating the truth into her pretty head.

"If Johnny doesn't make his shining goodness stand out there at the stockyards," said Gene, "Jordan would have made a big windy with the agent and not only had your steers released so they could be held out on the flats near his herd, but he manages to make himself look like a friend in your eyes. You and Banning hold your steers out on the flats waiting for the buyer to show up, and I think Jordan knew he wouldn't be here when you arrived, then your steers mysteriously disappear. You're broke, Banning is dead or hurt, and Jordan puts on a clean shirt and comes around to ask you to marry him."

"That adds up in my book," said Johnny huskily. "I sure do hanker to get my hands on Jordan, just him and me 'thout no interference. He's my meat, Gene, you hear?"

"You came near being his twice today," said Gene, "you don't want to crowd your luck. Not with Miss Micky depending on you."

"I depend on both of you," said Micky softly. "And I can see how you have put yourselves in danger for my sake. You promise me you'll be careful."

Johnny felt her words for him alone, and he squirmed in his saddle. "There's one thing still puzzles me, Gene," he said, trying to evade Micky's demand. "Jordan just naturally don't have the brains to figure out a scheme like thet."

"Will you be careful?" asked Micky.

"How about it, Gene?" asked Johnny. "Who is the think tank behind Jordan?"

Gene squinted at the Big Dipper before he answered. "Tell you when we finish planting a trap for these would-be rustlers," he said. "This night will run out on us if we don't quit gabbling. Here's what we have to do." Gene kneed Champ into a lope as he spoke.

Gene's plan to trap the Ladder rustlers was simple and clearly understood by the time they reached the Boxed H herd. Boomer was relieved to see Miss Hardesty ride up and it didn't take too long for him to see that she had found another friend in Gene. While he and Micky held the herd from spreading, Gene and Johnny worked quickly and surely.

Champ eased into the now standing steers and when Gene found the animal he wanted, one peculiarly marked or with a distinguishing deformity, like a missing horn, Champ slowly and patiently worked the animal to the edge of the herd where a sudden nudge of his shoulder broke the animal clear. While Champ kept him from turning back to the bunch, Gene dabbed his loop over the animal's head, stacked the dallies on the saddle horn and jerked the steer down in a helpless heap.

Johnny ran over with ready knife and knelt by the head of the hapless animal. There was a quick short bawl of anger, not pain, Johnny stuffed his hand in his pocket, found what he wanted, planted it, and jerked the noose off the steer's head.

The minute the steer was on his feet, Champ and Gene moved back in the bunch and started cutting out another. It was hard, fast, dangerous work but it was soon accomplished. Five of the most distinctive steers in the Boxed H herd carried the evidence that would convict Star Jordan and the Ladders of the deadly sin of rustling if they made the play that Gene expected.

Johnny was already beside Micky, talking to her in low tones when Gene reined up alongside.

"I'll leave you two alone in a minute," said Gene laughing, "but before I do, you listen to me. The Ladders will rustle this herd tonight; they have to if Jordan was telling anything like the truth about that buyer bein' here tomorrow. You don't get in their way at all, you understand?"

Johnny and Micky nodded.

"Miss Micky," said Gene, "I'm depending on you to make Banning behave and—" he paused.

"And what?" asked Micky breathlessly.

"And to keep Johnny close beside you," chuckled

Gene. "If he's got you to protect from flying lead, he won't be so apt to try to lick them singlehanded. Besides, we want those steers rustled by the Ladders." He wheeled Champ toward the distant lights of Hackberry when Johnny stopped him with a question.

"Before you ride off and leave me here twitching with curiosity, and just in case something sudden happens to you," said Johnny, "who is the brains behind Jordan's skulduggery?"

"I have a good idea, Johnny," said Gene, "but I don't want to put a name to my suspicions until I know they're right. There's a man that's said he would send for me to talk over a matter of mutual profit. I'm not waiting for him to send for me, I'm going to see him now. When I get through, I'll know. If I don't see you tomorrow morning, or sooner, it'll be because I can't. So long and take care of yourselves."

Champ stepped out briskly and Gene rode along into the night to face the man who perched on top of the Ladder.

A westbound freight was stopped beneath the water tower as Gene approached Hackberry from the Boxed H herd. He saw the fireman raise the water spout from the tender top. Far back along the line of cars, a pinpoint of lantern waved a highball that was acknowledged by a blast from the whistle. A rolling drumfire came from the stack as the engineer shoved the throttle bar hard over into the big hole.

A shower of sparks flew from the drivers as they churned against the rails and the metallic clang of metal against metal rippled down the line of cars as the slack came out of the couplings. The big Mogul compound had the train at full speed before the caboose cleared the dimly lighted station platform. The freight conductor standing on the rear steps of his "office" waved to the station agent as he rolled past.

Gene's eyes narrowed with sudden resolve. Using the horn of his saddle for a desk, Gene wrote quickly and clearly on a blank page of his tally book. He tore the leaf from the book, wrapped it around a cartridge from his belt to give it weight and plucked a long silky hair from Champ's mane to hold the message on its carrier. When he looked up from the finished task, the winking side lights of the caboose were flying down the track. Gene measured the distance and estimated the train speed with a practiced eye to pick his point of interception, and launched Champ through the night like a great arrow.

The conductor of the westbound freight was watching the station lights of Hackberry fade behind him when the noise of pounding hoofs came out of the night beside the train. He wheeled in startled surprise to see Champ pulling even with the caboose. Gene stood in the stirrups and made a careful underhand throw. A small heavy object thudded against the conductor's chest and dropped to the rocking rear platform of the caboose. It rolled toward the lip of the jolting platform and the startled conductor retrieved it just in time. He straightened up to see the horse and rider veer off into the night with a final wave from the rider's gloved hand.

The conductor was still blinking at the unexpected sight of a horse that could outrun a redball freight when he unwrapped the message from its leaden weight. He blinked again at the first words of Gene's note, read it through hastily and gulped. The message was addressed to the President of the Pacific Railroad. The conductor carefully placed the message with his train orders and wondered how soon he could get it despatched when he reached Barstow.

Champ was jogging easily across the tracks by the Hackberry station when Gene heard an excited voice.

"There he is," it cried.

Two figures were silhouetted by the station lights as they hastened toward him across the packed cinders. Gene signaled Champ to a halt as he recognized Pres Wesley and his smaller sidekick.

Pres came up with outstretched hand. "I done promised myself to shake your hand nex' time I saw you," he said. "Name of Wesley, Pres Wesley. This is my partner, Calvin Ellicott, otherwise known as Cal."

Gene took his hand without hesitation. "I'm Gene

Autry," he said, "Johnny Hines said you were a comfortable man in a tight place, and I can believe it after what you did to Nolan; and—" Gene shook with Cal in turn, "what your partner did to Jordan."

"Well," said Pres almost gaily, "I used to think I was fair to middlin' active with my brains but after watchin' you in action, I ain't so sure but what I'm gettin' too old for real troubled times."

"I hope not," said Gene seriously, "because things are apt to get real troubled right sudden like if Johnny and I have played the cards right. I'd feel better about it if I knew you weren't too old to lend a hand, Mr. Wesley. And your friend might keep a coffee cup handy too."

Pres grinned up at him. "I reckon I can make a hand if the need comes," he said. "And Cal here, why he'll do to take along. Just what brand of devilment are you hatchin' up behind that false front of bein' a saddle dude?"

"Where can I find Mr. J. Francis Gosslen?" asked Gene by way of answering the question.

Pres looked at him with a deepening respect on his face. "If you can pin that money-lending hyena to the wall," he said, "it'll surelee gladden my heart. Jordan, now, he's not much of a man but you can read what he is on his face and the way he acts. Gosslen gets fat off other folks' misfortunes with a pious look and a parson's speech, and his hands are as clammy as a toad in a well. You ain't aiming to plant a little dynamite under his house, are you?" asked Pres hopefully.

"Not the kind you're thinking of," said Gene. "I can't do anything real soon if you don't tell me where to find him."

Pres grinned again. "I talk a lot sometimes," he said. "You'll probably find Gosslen at his house sleeping the sleep of a man who feels that interest at ten per cent is his just reward."

"Where's that?" asked Gene impatient to get on with the night's work. The Big Dipper was ticking off the hours too fast to suit him.

Pres sensed the urgency in Gene's voice. "You hit the main street," he said, "and 'stead of turning toward the hotel, you turn left and follow along till the street runs out in sagebrush. Right there you'll see a little square house set off by itself with a picket fence around it. Only house in the Territory, I think, with a picket fence and it whitewashed to boot. Gosslen didn't build it," Pres added hastily. "He foreclosed it offen a lunger from back East who came out here for his health. Feller took too long gettin' well; borried from Old Piousness to keep goin'; Gosslen took the house and the man shot himself." Pres spat disgustedly.

"Where can I find you tonight in a hurry if I need someone to hold my hand in the dark?" asked Gene.

"Me and Cal'll be sleepin' down to the livery

stable yard," said Pres. "Up on top of the ore in my lead wagon with my rifle under my head. It's one good way to discourage people from stealing it out from under me. Besides," Pres looked down at Cal, "my partner here ain't never seen the morning star climb up above the rim of the world to the glory of the good Lord that made it."

Gene nodded understandingly. He felt the same way about the mystery and the glory of morning on the desert. This Pres Wesley was his kind of man.

"Yep," said Pres, "I really want Cal to have somethin' to tell his folks in California about."

"Do I have to go on the Limited tomorrow, Pres?" asked Cal with disappointment heavy in his question.

"I don't like it no better'n you do, Calico Cat," said Pres, "but we done sent that telegram to your folks over there that you'd been seein' America first and thet you'd be on tomorrow's train for sure. Yep, I guess it's got to be thetaway."

Gene looked down at Cal with a sudden twinkle in his eyes. "It may not be as tough as you think, Cal," he said. "California's not such a bad place if you know where to look and there are better ways of getting there than riding the cushions in a sleeping car."

Cal had a question or six poised on the tip of his tongue but when he looked up Gene wasn't there. He and Champ were turning down the main street to find the house of J. Francis Gosslen.

Pres watched him go for a long minute and then turned to Cal. "Come on, partner," said Pres Wesley, Esquire, "if we're goin' to do any sleepin' tonight, I got a hunch we better do it early in the evenin'—and it's kinda late now."

# CHAPTER EIGHT

Champ jogged down the street as light-footed as a boy in a melon patch. Gene had trained him well in this important feature. A light-footed horse was easy on his rider and on himself and there were times when it was essential that Champ's passing attract no attention. What little noise he made was muffled in the thick dust of the street.

The street wasn't long nor densely settled, Hackberry clustered toward its other end. Even so, the house Pres had described stood in splendid isolation where the street petered out into parallel ruts that quickly lost themselves in the sagebrush-dotted desert.

The Easterner who built it had kept his native ideas of architecture. The house was made of lumber instead of the 'dobe that was so cheap and comfortable. It sat well back from the street behind its incongruous picket fence, and wonder of wonders, Gene spotted a tall chimney rising from one end. The Easterner hadn't known that fireplaces weren't needed in this sun-drenched land. A great cottonwood outside the picket fence stretched long and

164

leafy branches toward the chimney end of the house.

Gene noticed all these things in his quick way and he noticed, too, that the location of the house made it possible for men to ride up to it from the desert and ride away again under cover of darkness with no one in Hackberry being any the wiser.

"Just like a spider web," he muttered grimly to himself, "and it reaches out over the whole Hualapai valley."

There was anticipation on Gene's face as he swung off Champ. His blood raced a little faster with the thrill of matching wits with the spider in the center of his web of evil. A gate opened through the picket fence and Gene thought swiftly about vaulting over it. Gates were apt to squeak. On second thought, he decided not to vault it. If the gate did squeak, Gosslen would know someone was coming to see him. He might make a false move that would cinch the matter of his guilt in Gene's mind. Gene pushed open the gate with a firm hand and it squeaked and squealed on hinges that needed a liberal dose of oil. Gene grinned to himself and strode quickly up the pathway.

The shades were drawn in the windows but little streamers of yellow lamplight poured out around their edges. Gene jumped lightly onto the porch and knocked loudly on the door. There was the sound of a chair being pushed back across the floor inside and footsteps approached the door in answer. Gene's keen ears caught the suspicion of other footsteps padding in another direction and the muffled sound of a door being closed inside the house. A locking bolt slid back, the front door opened inward and J. Francis Gosslen peered out.

"This is an unexpected pleasure, Mr. — Mr. — Dean," he said. "Come right in."

Gene's voice was wary. "You all alone, Mr. Gosslen?" he asked.

"Certainly," said Gosslen smoothly. He stepped back from the door in invitation. Gene swept off his hat as he crossed the threshold.

"Excuse me a moment," said Gosslen, shutting the door and stepping briskly around him, "I must complete these papers before I forget it." He seated himself at a plain deal table before the unused fireplace and busied himself importantly with several documents. Gene Autry took quick stock of his surroundings.

The room ran clear across the front of the house. It evidently served Gosslen as both living-room and office and it had no furniture to speak of besides a few plain chairs and Gosslen's desk with his cane laid across one end of it. A bookcase, partly filled with fat legal tomes, stood against one wall and a small iron safe was bolted to the floor in one corner behind the desk. A door led off the long, main room to other rooms in the rear of the house. Gene tried a ruse to see if Gosslen still had the visitors Gene suspected of

*Gosslen Busied Himself With Several Documents*

hiding upon his knock.

He grasped one of the chairs in his left hand and began to shove it across the floor toward Gosslen's desk. The lawyer looked up in annoyance at the noise and Gene, in seeming confusion, lifted the chair off the floor. A faint scuffle came from behind the door. Gene quickly lowered the chair and eased himself into it facing Gosslen as though he were sorry for the interruption.

Gosslen scratched his pen across the papers, waved them in the air for a moment and put them face down on the table. "The mice are eating me out of house and home," he said with a wan smile, "I hear them every night."

"You ought to find you a good cat," said Gene sympathetically. "Mice sure can be destructive. Why they don't care if people are around or not the way they carry on."

Gosslen smirked to himself at the ease with which his visitor swallowed this explanation of those scuffling noises. "What can I do for you?" he asked, looking at Gene under heavy-lidded eyes.

"I thought I'd come down and see you about that matter of mutual profit," said Gene easily. "I could use some money right now. I thought maybe you had something for me to do."

"I told you that I would send for you when I was ready," said Gosslen slowly as he grasped Gene's last remark.

"That's right, you did say that," said Gene. "I just thought we might get together before I had to move on—mebbe sudden like. Well, I'm sorry I bothered you, Mr. Gosslen." He started to rise from his chair ready to go but stopped at a wave from Gosslen's hand.

"As long as you're here," said Gosslen, "let me think of something."

Gene relaxed in his chair and seemed to be studying his boots. Gosslen made a steeple of his hands and pursed his lips reflectively while his mind clicked over like a well-oiled machine.

Thank goodness he was a thinking man, thought Gosslen to himself. He could always turn the unexpected to swift advantage. This dressed-up stranger was going to fit right into his plans. As a matter of fact, it almost seemed as though he had been sent by Gosslen's lucky stars at just the right moment. The stranger needed money and he might have to move on suddenly. These two remarks added to the stranger's actions during the day just passed added up perfectly to a logical conclusion. This man who called himself Dean was wanted by the law someplace for something.

No inkling of these thoughts nor of the diabolical plan behind them showed on Gosslen's face. If there was any expression there, it was that of a man trying hard to think of a way to do a stranger a good turn. Gosslen's face lighted up with sudden inspiration, and he cleared his throat to attract Gene's attention. He didn't realize it, but he had been the object of Gene's keen scrutiny all the time.

"There is a little matter you might be able to take care of for me until the bigger deal turns up," said Gosslen.

Gene's face showed his eagerness. "Give it a name," he said, "and I'm your man."

"It sounds like a very silly thing," said the lawyer mildly, "and I would hesitate to mention it except that I do like to help my friends." He paused and Gene seemed to twist impatiently in his chair. "Do you know where the young lady has her herd of steers bedded down?" asked Gosslen.

Gene nodded. "If you mean that wildcat that I just took out of the dining-room with that redheaded waddie, I sure do," he said.

"Well," said Gosslen and almost blushed, "our town marshal, Mr. Jordan, has an infatuation for that young lady. He doesn't feel any too happy about the way things have gone since she came to Hackberry at his request."

Gene bobbed his head in agreement. "I felt sorry for the marshal," he said. "That's why I helped him out there in the dining-room. I sure hope he appreciates it. I could use a good friend that's wearing a star."

Gosslen seemed to find this news no more than he had expected. "I will certainly tell the marshal my own opinion of your quick thinking," he said oilily. "That is one reason why I feel sure we can work together in helping out the marshal's courtship of Miss Hardesty."

"Anything I can do to get even with her for quirting me off that redhead will be a pleasure," said Gene vindictively.

Gosslen nodded. "I thought you would feel that way," he said. "Now here is what I want you to do. The young lady intends to drive her steers up the valley to Hines's homestead as soon as they sign the papers that makes Hines surety for the railroad watering charges. I want you to run off their extra saddle horses and pack mules so they will not be able to move out as they now plan."

Gene's excited voice cut him off in mid-sentence. "No, sir," he said positively, "I won't steal horses for any man or any money. Not even to get square with that girl."

Gosslen's face showed pained surprise. "No one is asking you to be a horse thief," he said soothingly. "You didn't let me finish my explanation."

Gene seemed unconvinced. "Man runs off another man's horse, he's a horse thief," he said stubbornly.

"Ordinarily, I might agree with you," said Gosslen patiently, "but this is no ordinary case. If you will not interrupt, Mr. Dean, I am sure that I can show you this matter in its true light."

"You go right ahead," said Gene, "but it better be

good to change my mind."

"You run off the spare horses," said Gosslen, "and drive them down the valley. You'll see a windmill there when daylight comes if you have made good speed. Pen the horses in the windmill corral and ride back to Hackberry."

"That's still horse stealing," said Gene, "and I won't have any part of it. Men get hung for that a whole lot quicker than they do for rustling, or robbery, or house burning. No, sir, it doesn't appeal to me at all."

Gosslen was as patient as a snake waiting at the mouth of a prairie dog hole. "After you get back to Hackberry," he said ignoring Gene's outburst, "the marshal will ride out with several of his men. They will find the horses where you have left them, and return them to Miss Hardesty. This will give the marshal a chance to gain more favorable consideration in her eyes. Really, Mr. Dean, you are getting a chance to play Cupid on horseback." Gosslen smiled in self-amusement.

Gene seemed to be convinced by this line of reasoning and nodded his head slowly. Suddenly he shook it violently. "Wait a minute," he said. "That all sounds fine when you're sitting behind a desk in a nice comfortable house in town. What happens to me if that red-muzzled son-of-a-man-named-Hines spots me prowling around out there? Hey? Or suppose that sawed-off old Texan catches me in the sights of his rifle? You saw him load it yourself, and there's just enough moon and starshine for him to take a bead with. No, sir, Mr. Gosslen, you make a good talk but talk's not enough."

Gosslen rose from his chair and knelt before the safe behind his desk. The dial clicked around, spun back and clicked again. Gosslen grunted as he tugged open the surprisingly thick door. His hands were busy inside the safe for a moment, then he rose to his feet and faced Gene with his hand outstretched.

"Does this talk loud enough, Mr. Dean?" he asked. Five round, yellow, double-eagles gleamed in the soft lamplight. "One hundred dollars gold is very good pay for a night's work, a half-night really," said Gosslen. "And don't forget, Mr. Dean, that you might want to move on—*kinda sudden like,* I think you said. Could it be, Mr. Dean, that the marshal, or even a plain citizen like myself could make a handsome sum in reward money by preventing you from ever moving on permanently?" There was no mistaking the menace in Gosslen's voice.

Gene lowered his eyes to hide the sudden exultation that leaped into them. Gosslen had fallen for his veiled hints and thought he was on the dodge from the law someplace else. The man was so sure of his own intelligence that he believed what he wanted to believe without checking it.

"I'll do it," said Gene sullenly, "Give me the

money." He reached out a hand.

Gosslen saw his suspicions confirmed and took his usual cold-blooded advantage of anyone who fell within his power. "You get the money when you get back to Hackberry," he sneered. "Do you think I am a complete fool? You'd take the money and ride off without living up to your side of the bargain. Oh, no, Mr. Whatever-Your-Name-Is, I pay when the job is done."

Gene seemed completely cowed by Gosslen's threats to expose him to the law. "I better get started," he said, and rose heavily to his feet. "This night's running out and I sure don't want to get caught messing around those horses in daylight." He walked slowly toward the door and Gosslen padded after him smiling thinly in satisfaction.

Gene opened the door and stepped through it to stop and turn toward Gosslen. "I ought to have some of that money before I start," he said doggedly. "How do I know you won't double-cross me when I get back—or turn me in anyway?"

"You don't," said Gosslen grimly. "You do what I want done and you get your money. If you do it right, there will be other jobs that pay much more. It depends on you."

Gene seemed to turn this ultimatum over in his mind and let a look of relief steal across his face. "I'll be rocking along, Mr. Gosslen," he said quickly.

Gosslen interpreted the look on Gene's face just

as Gene had intended that he would. "If you have any notion that you can ride out of Hackberry and keep moving on," said Gosslen with a purr in his voice, "let me advise you against it."

Gene looked crestfallen.

"You see," said Gosslen, "we have a very efficient means of preventing men from leaving our organization. If you are not back in Hackberry by midday tomorrow—" Gosslen's voice died away significantly and he shrugged his shoulders as if disclaiming any responsibility for what would happen to Gene.

"I'll be back, Mr. Gosslen," said Gene hastily. "Yes, sir, I certainly will be back. The more I see of your way of handling things, the more I want to see—" Gene stopped short. "What's that?" he barked. The noise of horses riding out of the desert beyond the house had come faintly to his ears.

"I have no idea," said Gosslen. "Perhaps you should get started before some chance passer-by sees you here."

"I'm on my way," said Gene, "and, Gosslen, do you see what I see?" Gene pointed toward his hand with his chin, Indian fashion. Gosslen looked and nodded silently. A long-barreled six-gun was in Gene's hand and the muzzle pointed squarely at Gosslen's belt buckle. "I don't know how it got there," said Gene quietly, "but, Gosslen, let me make you one small promise true. It can get there again. Don't try to deal yourself all the aces in this little game of yours."

The sound of approaching horses was drawing toward the back of the house. "I'll see you tomorrow and collect," said Gene.

He jumped out of the light from the door into the yard and ran toward the picket fence, whistling for Champ to meet him. The fact that Gosslen had lied about being alone, coupled with the approaching riders, spurred Gene to a fever pitch. Gosslen was gathering the Golden Ladder gang for orders and Gene intended to learn what those orders were. Also, just how Gosslen planned to involve his proposed Cupid's errand in the scheme of things.

He vaulted the picket fence without breaking his stride and saw Champ running toward him, whinnying softly. Gene leapfrogged into the saddle. Quickly he unfastened the long riata and slid his arm through the coils until they were snug against his shoulder. He squeezed Champ with his knees and was standing in the saddle when Champ plunged beneath an overhanging branch of the great cottonwood that gave shade to Gosslen's house.

Gene gave a cat jump into the air and grasped the rough-barked limb. Champ pounded on into the night apparently toward Hackberry and Gene pulled himself up and onto the limb behind the protecting screen of leaves. The sound of Champ's pounding feet seemed to die away in the dust and Gene smiled to himself at the results of long hours of training that had made him a true champion among horses.

The rattle of stirrups and the creak of saddle leather behind Gosslen's house indicated the arrival of the riders out of the desert. Gene moved quickly to take advantage of the noise they would undoubtedly make when they entered Gosslen's back door.

Gene made his careful way along the great limb that reached out from the cottonwood toward Gosslen's chimney. He chuckled to himself as he thought about the remarks people sometimes made about the length of a California riata, a skin string the tie-hard waddies called it. The one Gene carried was eighty feet long and as perfect as skillful hands could make it. He slid the coils down off of his shoulder and with one quick whirl, he sent the noose snaking out across the night to loop the chimney and be snapped tight before the heavy rawhide hondo could clatter down against the roof. He tied the loose end of the riata with a special knot to a shorter limb above the one on which he stood. Balancing precariously on one foot, then on the other, he carefully pried off his boots and tied them to the loose end of the riata. He lowered them until the slack was all paid out and the boots swung slowly to and fro high enough above the ground to prevent a chance passer-by from hitting them but not too high to be reached by a man standing on the back of a horse about the same size as Champ.

Gene grasped the riata above his head with both

hands, swung his legs over it so the line ran under the crooks of his knees and carefully slid himself along its length until his hat pressed gently against the chimney stones. The men who had ridden up out of the night were just entering Gosslen's house. Their careless, noisy entry masked the faint sounds that Gene made in transferring himself from the riata to the chimney and then dropping panther-like to the roof. He seemed to melt into the chimney itself and the voices from the room below traveled up the flue from the fireplace as if coming up a speaking tube.

"Yuh shore took yuh're time augurin' with thet pilgrim," said Jordan's heavy tones. "Me'n Nolan like tuh bust out laughin' when yuh started yammerin' about mice. They ain't been a mouse in this house since yuh moved in, Gosslen. They plumb starved tuh death." Jordan laughed huskily at his joke.

"I had good reason for persuading Mr. Dean to see things my way," said Gosslen icily. "They were reasons that will help you to keep that paunch of yours in its present swollen state, my fat marshal. Are all your men here?"

"Six of 'em," said Jordan. "Thet's whut yuh said we'd need."

"Very well," said Gosslen. "Listen carefully to your instructions. Marshal Jordan here," Gosslen's voice was filled with restrained fury, "has done his

*Gene Slid Himself Along to the Chimney*

blundering best to destroy my plans at least three times today. I want no slip-ups tonight. This is the biggest undertaking I have yet contrived and it will bring rich rewards to all of you." He paused dramatically and a little ripple of greedy exclamations floated up the chimney from the assembly in the room below.

The reaction of his followers was not lost upon Gosslen as Gene could tell from his voice, when he continued his instructions.

"First come the Boxed H steers," said Gosslen, confident that their greed would bend their bodies to do his will. "It is a small return for the trouble involved but absolutely essential to Jordan's happiness. You six men will surround the Boxed H herd and drive the steers into the Ladder cattle below them on the flats. Stampede them, yell, whoop, make it sound like bronco Apaches raiding but do not kill anyone unless it is absolutely necessary. I detest violence."

"Whut'll we do with thuh girl?" asked a voice unknown to Gene.

"Yuh be mighty careful with her," growled Jordan.

"More specifically," said Gosslen, "you will capture her, blindfold her, and take her wherever Jordan tells you to take her. That is no concern of mine. And Jordan," his voice cracked like a whip, "I don't want to hear what you tell your men. That is entirely your business and don't forget either, that I get all the money from the sale of her steers as well as my usual share from the other cattle for being the thinking partner in the Ladders. You understand?"

"That's thuh deal we made," said Jordan, "an' I shore got thuh best of it." He laughed coarsely and Gene's blood ran cold, then hot, at the sound.

"You are entitled to your own opinion, Marshal," said Gosslen, "and I hope you do not regret it. Personally, I have found brains better than brawn but, of course, you have never had the chance to prove this for yourself."

Jordan's surly voice started to reply to Gosslen's contemptuousness.

"Shut up," snapped Gosslen. "I hold you in the hollow of my hand, Jordan, and you know it. If anything happens to me, a sealed envelope will be opened by a trusted friend of mine a long way from here. Do you want that to happen, Marshal Jordan? You don't?" Gosslen's voice was scornful. "Then see to it that nothing does happen to me, Marshal Star Jordan, and keep your mouth shut while I am talking.

"The six men who rustle the Boxed H steers get a double share for their risk," continued Gosslen. "The overdressed stranger who calls himself Dean will have run off their loose horses by the time you come on the scene and they may be stirred up over this misfortune. On the other hand, they may be scattered out looking for them and thus give you little opposition. Do everything possible to make it look like the work of Indians off the reservation, or renegade whites. Now, Jordan, step outside and tell your men what it is you want them to do with the girl."

The noise of booted feet scuffling toward the rear door floated up the chimney. Gene was about to cover his departure with their noise when Gosslen's voice made him freeze in his tracks.

"Have them watch outside until I finish with you and Nolan," said Gosslen.

Gene was faced with a terrible decision. He had counted on making his getaway when the meeting broke up. Now, Gosslen's last words to Jordan made it essential that he stay on the roof to learn what other plans were afoot. If he stayed, the men just assigned to patrol outside the house might spot him on the roof top. Or they might blunder into Champ who he knew had returned to the vicinity of the cottonwood to await his master's signal. If they spotted him or Champ, he might die right there in a circle of deadly fire.

If he died or were captured, the Boxed H herd and its guardians were doomed, either to death or worse. Should he leave now while he had the chance and thus make sure that the Boxed H got warning? Or should he stay where he was to learn what other crooked schemes Gosslen had in mind for Jordan and his gunman, Nolan? Gene analyzed the situation with a wry grin on his handsome face but there was no hesitation in picking his course of action. He knew what he had to do and he did it.

# CHAPTER NINE

## SAWING THE RUNGS

Gene stayed at his self-imposed post of duty even though his life hung in the balance. He was determined to bring the Ladder gang to justice. To do this, he had to know what else Gosslen had afoot.

If he were discovered, he would trust to the luck of the fighting man to get him through in safety. If he did not win through, he would at least throw Gosslen's plans off schedule. If he didn't show up tomorrow morning, Johnny would know that he had gone under and would take good care to protect himself and Micky. Gene flattened himself against the chimney with his hat crumpled under his arm and played out the hand Fate had dealt him.

He could not make out Jordan's words as he gave his orders to the men who were to kidnap Micky but there was no mistaking the gloating evil in his voice. Gene heard the back door click shut as Jordan went inside and the Ladder riders fanned out to watch the house on all sides. Gene fixed their locations in his mind and then almost bent an ear as Gosslen's voice floated up the chimney.

"We can get down to business now," said Gosslen

briskly. "A much more profitable venture than a few steers and a pretty girl. This opportunity stems entirely from my observing habits. For example, from the time the westbound Limited whistles at the mouth of Dead Horse Canyon until it stops in Hackberry for water, the time is exactly fourteen and one-half minutes. Did either of you know that?"

"Naw," said Jordan disgustedly, "an' whut difference does it make? We got other things tuh do besides listen tuh train whistles."

"If you would listen to them, Jordan," said Gosslen acidly, "it might keep you from trying to think for yourself. However, I used the Limited whistle to show you what an observing man can learn about everyday things around him. I have learned a great deal about our worthy merchant, Herman Gerbode—"

"Dum' Dutchman," rumbled Jordan.

"Perhaps you are right," said Gosslen, "but what concerns us now is the simple fact that Gerbode is a creature of very methodical habit. He opens his dining-room precisely at six o'clock every morning to feed his railroad boarders who go to work at seven. He does not open his store until eight o'clock.

"While his dumpy wife feeds the hungry, Gerbode spends those two hours getting the store ready for business. First, he closes the door from the dining-room to the store so he will not be interrupted. He then sweeps the store, unlocks the back door, carries the trash outside, goes back inside, leaving the back door unlocked and spends the rest of the time putting stock on the shelves and otherwise preparing for business. I have spent some time observing Gerbode's routine and it never varies." There was an air of conscious superiority in Gosslen's voice as though he were above such humdrum ways of earning a living.

"Whut's thet got to do with us?" growled Jordan. "We ain't goin' tuh help him."

"Yes, we are!" snapped Gosslen. "Nolan is going to help him directly and you, Jordan, are going to help him too."

"Long's I git paid," said Nolan's flat tones, "I'll do anythin'. I ain't proud if the *dinero* is waitin' fer me."

"Thank goodness, you are sensible," purred Gosslen. "There will be more money than you ever saw before waiting for all of us tomorrow morning. And," he continued smugly, "it will be easy to take and without risk, thanks to my powers of observation."

"Let's hear it," said Nolan and Jordan grumbled something that Gene couldn't quite catch. It sounded as though Jordan didn't want Gosslen to hear him but had to mutter to himself like a spanked child.

"Tomorrow morning," said Gosslen as if he were assigning a lesson in class, "Gerbode will go through his usual routine. Nolan will be hiding at the back of the building in the alley with a red-colored horse saddled and gleaming with silver.

"Ain't got no silver-mounted gear," interposed Nolan.

"You can make it," said Gosslen curtly. "Use pieces cut out of tin cans. They glitter in the sunlight and you can throw them away without any sense of loss afterward.

"When Gerbode goes inside after dumping his sweepings," continued Gosslen, "he always unpacks cases to stock his shelves. Tomorrow morning, I am sure that he will unpack a case of dry goods first of all. The case of dry goods will contain the currency supply for the opening of the Bank of Hackberry." His voice curled in anger.

"Nolan will see me come up the street and enter your office, Jordan. That is his signal. He will use the unlocked back door, wearing a mask. Nolan will take the larger denominations only, stuff them into a grain sack (there are plenty of them around the store), lock Gerbode in his own bank corner, with no violence unless necessary. You understand that he is not to be killed, Nolan?"

"Why not?" came the cold-blooded question.

"Because, you fool, it is unnecessary," snapped Gosslen. "He will not recognize you behind that mask, and even if he began to suspect you as the robber, Jordan and I will throw him off the scent."

"How?" grunted the marshal.

"Listen and don't talk so much," said Gosslen irritably. "Nolan then walks out the back door, closes it, steps around the corner, swings into the saddle and rides at full speed down the alley and across the street. He will drag a saddle blanket behind him to raise plenty of dust. Any chance citizen walking the street will see only a masked rider on a red horse glittering with silver trappings. Nolan rides past your office, Jordan, and throws the sack in the open door. I get the sack and transfer the money to my brief case. I always carry a brief case when I come to see you on legal matters, Marshal Jordan, as you will conveniently remember.

"Nolan rides across the tracks and makes for the Ladder herd where he has been all the time as a dutiful strawboss. The mask is dropped, the tin ornaments are torn off and become nothing but pieces of tin can. I walk out of your office and naturally head for the dining-room to see if you are there having breakfast, Marshal."

"I don't generally eat there," said Jordan, "and not that early."

"You will eat there that early tomorrow morning," said Gosslen without hesitation. "Gerbode will set up a howl the minute he thinks it is safe. You will hear the noise, Marshal, and take your time getting him out. By the time you get his story about the robber, (he will undoubtedly scream in his usual broken English) Nolan will be safe at the Ladder herd where he can attend to the Boxed H steers.

"Nolan, as soon as that job is completed, bring the whole herd to the stockyards to wait for the buyer. You hear about the bank robber and send the men out to look for him. They, thus, have ample time to confuse their tracks of the night before.

"In the meantime, Jordan, I will be attracted by Gerbode's fuss and join you together with what other townspeople are around. Gerbode will be unable to describe the robber except in general terms. By a happy coincidence," Gosslen's voice was smug, "Nolan and the stranger named Dean are about the same general build. If any of the towns-people saw Nolan cross the street in a cloud of dust, they will all be eager to describe what they saw—a masked rider, a silver saddle.

"It will be my duty as a citizen to chime in with the fact that I was looking out your office window when I saw the same thing. You, Marshal Jordan, will ask where the man Dean is. Nobody knows. You then point the finger of suspicion at him. Sorrel horse, silver saddle, same build, and I will add fuel to the flames by admitting that the masked rider did remind me of Dean. You, Jordan, will then ride out gallantly to overtake him. No posse will be needed because there isn't time to stop and raise one."

"Thet sounds slick as silk," rasped Nolan, "but whut if this Dean shows up?"

"That is the beauty of my little scheme," said Gosslen. "Dean has gone to rustle the Boxed H horses and drive them down to the windmill in the valley. I promised him a handsome reward for his work and he was very eager to oblige me. The marshal will ride toward the windmill in hot pursuit of the bank robber. Dean will be riding back toward Hackberry to collect his pay and the marshal will give it to him."

"Me pay him?" sputtered the bewildered marshal. "Whut with?"

"With that shoulder gun you wear," snapped Gosslen. "What could be more natural than for you to see a man on a sorrel horse with a handsome silver saddle riding down the valley. You give chase, because the bank robber rode this kind of an outfit. The rider fires at you. You kill him for resisting an officer of the law."

"Yes, but—" said Jordan.

"Don't sound so puzzled," said Gosslen patiently. "Dean will ride up to you expecting your friendship thanks to my missionary work with him. You simply shoot him before he knows what's happened to him and bring his body into Hackberry tied across his handsome saddle. Great acclaim for Marshal Jordan in getting the bandit so quickly. Too bad he had a chance to hide the money before you caught him. He must have had a confederate. Who could it be? What more natural than the Boxed H people? They get arrested for questioning and if necessary, they get killed for resisting arrest. The money is never found and Hackberry has a buried treasure legend to tell Eastern visitors." Gosslen laughed at his own wry humor and Gene felt a ripple of cold rage race up his spine.

There was a long silence in the room below as Jordan and Nolan digested the master plan of J. Francis Gosslen. Gene looked at the Big Dipper and saw that he had been on the roof for more than an hour. The night was past its midpoint and things would have to happen fast.

Gene grinned at the thought. Things were apt to happen fast as soon as he started to leave the roof. A dog barked in the distance, an inquiring sort of bark that changed to the excited yelping that a cat chase brings out in the most dignified dog. Gene grinned another friendly grin at this remembered sound and stiffened rigidly at the next words that came up from the chimney.

"Just whut happens to thet money?" asked Jordan.

"After you ride off in search of the bandit," said Gosslen, "I will sympathize with Gerbode and offer him my assistance. Then I will pick up my brief case and walk calmly down the street to my house—this house. The money will be deposited in that safe you see in the corner and *there it stays until the time comes to divide it.*"

"Whut makes yuh so shore thet Nolan won't keep a'ridin' with thuh sack 'stid of throwin' it to yuh?"

asked Jordan suspiciously.

"Nolan is too intelligent to try that," purred Gosslen. "Nolan knows which side his bread is buttered on. Don't you, Nolan?" Gosslen's voice was more threat than question.

"Nolan will have another incentive to play fair with us," continued Gosslen amiably, "because Nolan will get a full share in the Ladder outfit if he does his job well. I have the papers drawn up. See— here they are. How does that strike you, Nolan?"

"I ain't much fer talkin'," Nolan's voice was clipped. "I do my job an' I get my share. If I don't, there'll be blood on the moon."

"I don't like it," said Jordan. "It's too tricky. If thet money's down to Gerbode's store why don't we gather the boys an' ride down there and get it now 'stid of all this play-actin'?"

Gosslen's voice showed that he was at the ragged edge of his patience. "I often wonder why I ever let myself become involved with such stupidity as yours, Jordan," he gritted. "The simple stratagem I have just outlined in words of one syllable leaves us all in the clear with a perfect victim and no questions. Dean is killed resisting arrest. His ostensible confederates are jailed or killed and the secret of the stolen money dies with them. If the money disappears from Gerbode's store in the middle of the night, suspicion can fasten upon any one of us. There will be no more argument. Either we do it as planned, or we abandon the project entirely. There is a lot of money in that case!"

Gosslen waited for a moment to let this thought sink home. He must have been satisfied with what he saw on the faces of Jordan and Nolan.

"Ah," said Gosslen, "you cannot bear the thought of losing so much easy money, can you? Very well, we'll proceed as planned. Now, you had better be on your way."

The noise of two men pushing back their chairs as they rose to their feet gave Gene his cue to take the desperate chance of escape that was open to him. Very cautiously, he slid the noose of the riata up the chimney and thanked his stars for the fact that rawhide had more stretch to it than grass rope. Carefully he worked the noose free of the chimney until he held it firmly in both muscular hands. He was almost ready to jump when a final slice of information made him pause.

"Thet station agent was askin' me when he's goin' tuh get his money fere helpin' us play thet little joke on the Boxed H's down to the stockyards," said Jordan.

"He will not get a penny," snapped Gosslen. "That poor fool served our purpose because he was hungry to make a dollar or two extra. The joke will be on him. He will be my tool at any time I choose to use him in the future because he will be afraid of losing his job with the railroad if I reveal his part in those trumped up watering charges to his superiors."

"Yuh can handle him then," said Jordan. "That kind of persuasion is more in yore line."

What else Gosslen or Jordan or Nolan might have said or done was lost to Gene right then and there. The dog that he had heard pick up the delightful scent of cat was in full cry and drawing closer and closer to Gosslen's house.

The watching riders moved their horses cautiously toward the sound and bunched together at the back of the picket fence. There was nervous talk among them and the horses stirred restlessly.

The dog ceased his baying for a brief space of time and then broke out with redoubled fury almost on top of the clustered gunmen. A horse spooked and then swallowed his head in fright. One quick shot tore the night apart and the dog howled in mortal agony. The men inside the house moved toward the back door and a sudden scrambling noise on the roof made Gene's blood race faster.

He had no time to figure out what caused the noise because the noise explained itself. A hissing, spitting bundle of fur with claws like razor blades ran up his leg, clawed its way to his shoulder and jumped from the feel of flesh beneath its paws onto the lip of the chimney.

No house cat ever made that throaty snarl and Gene's lips twitched at the corners. Before the surprised bobcat knew what had happened, Gene's gloved hand closed around its neck close behind its flat-eared head.

"You better go down and catch those two-legged mice of Gosslen's," he said quietly and dropped the bobcat down the chimney.

Frantic snarls, mingled with curses and wild confusion came from the room below. Gene didn't wait to hear what happened. The luck of the fighting man had come to him and he took swift advantage of it.

He grasped the riata with both hands as far out as he could reach. He arched his powerful shoulders and pushed swiftly with both feet. The riata swung down across the night like a giant pendulum. At the top of its swing, Gene jumped as far as he could with the hope that there was no cactus below him.

The noise of the riata swishing against the cottonwood branches went unnoticed in the furor inside the house. The riders at the back had swarmed inside to help out and the bobcat was giving them all a run for their money.

Gene whistled softly for Champ and breathed a sigh of relief when the horse materialized out of the darkness. Once in the saddle, Gene retrieved his boots and jerked the slip knot of the riata free. Then he wheeled Champ toward Hackberry, coiling up the rawhide as he rode. There was much to be done and too little time to do it unless everything went like clockwork.

The faint glow from a night lantern inside the stables gave Gene ample light to pick out Pres Wesley's wagon. Gene grinned to himself and lifted his voice in soft melodious song.

> *Wake up, Jacob,*
> *Day's a'breakin',*
> *Coffee's hot,*
> *An' hoe cake bakin'.*

There was a cautious stirring of blankets on top of the wagon and Pres poked a tousled head gingerly over the towering side boards.

"I never heard no round-up cook sing it so sweet before," said Pres, "but you sound just as cheerful as any belly-robber disturbing hard workin' men. Shucks, it's way before breakfast. What's on your mind?"

"Steer rustling, kidnaping and bank robbery," said Gene. "That enough to make you rise and shine?"

"It's right close to bein' too much," said Pres as he swung his feet over the wagon side. "How, when, and where are the next questions?"

"No time to argue all the unpleasant details," said Gene briskly. "I been prowling around the roof of J. Francis Gosslen's and it's due to happen right suddenlike. Can you collect a few reliable citizens to side you and powder up to Gerbode's to wait till I get back from the Boxed H's?"

*"What's on Your Mind?" Asked Pres*

Pres scratched his head. "You're askin' a whole lot, especially this time of mornin'," he said. "Reeliable citizens is what Hackberry ain't got, not the kind you mean. Howsomever, Gerbode did say that he was expectin' 'Relio Baca to come into town for the bank openin' tomorrow and 'Relio is plumb reeliable. He can shoot a lizard's eye out as far as he can see him."

"There won't be any shooting," said Gene, "not if we play it smart. What we need is somebody whose word is good, anytime, anyplace, anywhere."

" 'Relio qualifies for that," said Pres. "Let's go find him."

"You go," ordered Gene. "I have to get word to the Boxed H's first."

"That's goin' to take time," said Press. "Why don't we send Cal here out with a message?"

"Too much risk," said Gene shaking his head. "Besides, Johnny Hines might not believe him. You know Baca and I don't. Baca knows you and he doesn't know me. The same for Gerbode. You collect Baca, if he's in town, and I'll meet you in the store soon as I can make it. Tell you the play then. One thing more, can we get to the roof from inside the store?"

Pres nodded. "Yep, sure can," he said, and began to pull on his high freighter's boots. He lifted his head as if a thought had just occurred to him. "Suppose you don't get back, how do we know what's coming or what we're to do?"

Gene saw the reason behind this question. "If I don't make it before time for Gerbode to open for business," said Gene firmly, "you be hiding in the store and you drill any strange jasper that shows up, even if he looks like me."

"That ought to be easy," said Pres. "Come on, Calico Cat, let's take our foot in our hand. We got work to do."

Pres suited action to his words by using the high rear wheel for a ladder to the ground and his long rifle came with him. By the time Cal joined him, Gene and Champ were trotting out of the wagon-yard behind the stables.

Gene slowed Champ to an easy trot before they came to the Boxed H herd. No sense in riding pell mell out of the night and spooking the cattle. More to the point, Johnny and Banning might shoot first and ask questions later. Gene pushed his hat back on his head and his voice sang through the night.

*Old J. Johnny Hines was a plumb total loss;*
*He courted his girl on a sway-back hawss.*
*That hawss he bucked and off Hines fell,*
*His girl married me 'cause I ride so well.*
*Now poor Johnny Hines, his heart was broke,*
*He never was able to take a joke,*
*But me and the girl, we thought it was swell*
*While poor Johnny Hines went to Stovepipe Well.*

"I did not," came Johnny's voice out of the darkness. "Can't you quit botherin' a fellow on night guard with them mournful caterwauls?"

"Why, Johnny," said Gene, "are you still awake? I thought you'd be sound asleep on your Tucson bed by now."

"What's a Tucson bed?" asked Johnny, his curiosity getting the best of him.

"Why, that's a bed you make by lying on your back and covering it with your stomach," said Gene. "You ought to try it sometime."

Micky Hardesty's tinkling laughter increased Johnny's embarrassment.

"Aw, Gene," said Johnny. "Quit joshin' me. What's on yore mind? I know you didn't come out here just to sing us a lullaby."

Gene's voice reflected his seriousness. "Not altogether, I didn't," he agreed, "but it was one good way of keeping you from mistaking me for Jordan."

"Yore right," said Johnny getting even. "Not even Jordan could sound like that."

"He sure couldn't," said Gene, "and he wouldn't like these sounds either. Things are coming to a head quick and lively. I found out everything I needed to know and now you and Boomer have to play your parts."

"Give us your powders," said Johnny.

"You and Boomer take the loose horses and fog 'em down the valley till good daylight," said Gene.

"Then start hazing 'em back toward town. You'll meet Star Jordan pursuing a silver-mounted bank robber and he'll be some surprised to find you instead of me. Don't give him a chance to ask questions. Tell him somebody run off your horses in the night. You split up to find 'em. When you found 'em, Miss Hardesty's riderless horse was with 'em. Have her horse right there so's he can see it."

"But what—" began Micky.

"Come to that in a minute," said Gene. "Tell Jordan you think 'Paches got her, tell him anything you can think of, only don't let him get back to town too soon. Argue with him, demand that he find Micky, do whatever you can to hold him without makin' him suspicious that you aren't telling him the gospel truth. Jordan's not going to be too eager to find that bank robber, meaning me, when he sees Micky's horse. He's goin' to be plumb eager to sell his Ladder herd to the buyer that's due to arrive come morning and get out to wherever he's told his men to stash Micky. When he drags his freight, you and Boomer slide up to the stockyards and wait for me, or something else to happen. Savvy?"

Johnny knew Gene's voice from past experience. "Savvy," he said, "only I got a sinkin' feelin' that I'm goin' to miss all the fun."

"You just remember," said Gene, "that you wouldn't promise to be careful when Miss Micky asked you. I had to promise to look out for you."

Johnny snorted.

"But, Gene," said Micky Hardesty, "if Johnny and Boomer ride away, what happens to my steers? And what happens to me?" Micky still wasn't used to being told what to do.

"Your steers are going to end up wearing the Ladder brand before morning," said Gene, "and that's exactly what we want to happen, to trap the Ladder gang so they can't get out of it."

Gene kneed Champ over alongside Micky's horse and lifted himself out of the saddle to a seat on Champ's rump. "Now," said Gene, "you slide over into Champ's saddle and you and me will ride back to Hackberry."

"I don't have to," snapped Micky, disliking the idea of leaving her steers.

"Miss Micky," said Gene, "I need your riderless horse to convince Jordan that his part of the plan has gone okay. And I want you safe in Gerbode's hotel just to keep it from panning out the way it's supposed to."

"But I still don't understand what all this fuss is about," said Micky, "and—"

Gene's strong arms plucked Micky from her horse and placed her firmly in the saddle before him. "When we have more time," said Gene, "Johnny can explain it to you and what he doesn't know he can make up. That is, unless he's become a changed man since he met you."

"I shore have," said Johnny earnestly, "but that won't stop me from explainin' a lot of things at the right time." The message in his voice was plain.

Gene wasted no more time in argument. Champ moved into the night.

"See you at the stockyards, Johnny," said Gene, and Champ hit a high lope before Micky had a chance to say any more.

# CHAPTER TEN

### RED-HANDED

Gene fetched a wide circle to enter Hackberry in the opposite direction from the Boxed H herd. Time was running out on him, a lighter band of sky already outlined the jagged eastern peaks and the morning star was winking bravely high above them, but the longest way round was the safest. Gene had to play it safe. With Micky in the saddle before him, he could not run the risk of meeting Ladder riders on the prowl and expose her to possible gun play.

The longest way round should have been the sweetest for Micky except for one thing. Micky Hardesty was accustomed to giving orders, not taking them, and she thought of the scorching things she would say to this high-handed Gene Autry to put him in his place.

Champ's effortless gait ate up the distance like fire. He had covered a whale of a lot of country since morning and now he was carrying double in a race against time. If he or Gene were tired, they didn't show it. The perfect physical condition of man and horse were factors that really counted when the going got tough and justice depended on their ability to balance the scales against evil and oppression.

The glow of the night lantern in the feed corrals was paling before the onrushing dawn when Gene slid from Champ's back and helped Micky to the ground. She swayed with weariness and Gene half-caught her in his arms and helped her to a seat on a feed box. He unsaddled Champ with practiced speed, wiped him down and led him inside a box stall at the far end of the stables. Then he covered his saddle and gear with loose hay to conceal them from prying eyes and helped Micky to the back door of Gerbode's store.

Pres must have been waiting right there because Gene had no more than knocked once when the door swung open and Pres's anxious face greeted him.

"I'm surelee glad you got here," said Pres. "I been as nervous as a tree full of chickadees." He closed the door behind them.

"First off," said Gene, "we have to get Miss Hardesty here a safe place to sleep." Micky was leaning against him with weariness.

Gerbode bustled out of the room yelling for his wife. Mrs. Gerbode, a plump woman with a seamed and kindly face, took charge of Micky with a motherly gesture and Hermie's pride in his wife was reflected in his voice as the two women left the store. "Momma dakes goot gare off her, you pets," said Hermie.

Pres momentarily took charge of the little gathering by saying, "This is Gene Autry, no matter what other names he goes by. Gene, this is Hermie Gerbode and Aurelio Baca."

Gerbode bobbed his head in acknowledgment and Baca swept off his dun-colored sombrero with a flourish. "This is a great honor," he said softly.

Gene studied him with an increased interest as he realized the excellence of his English. The *hacendado* was a compactly built man of middle height, powerful without fat, and dressed in the usual garb of the desert rider. His only concessions to the traditions of his ancestors were a broad maroon sash that served him instead of belt and a tight-fitting jacket of dark cloth handsomely embroidered with silver thread. His face was a square frame with high cheekbones and an imperious nose offset by two merry blue eyes beneath thick brows. A mop of red hair completed the picture and Gene liked what he saw.

"If you two'll get finished inspectin' one another," said Pres dryly, "mebbe Gene can tell us what the play is."

Gene grinned fleetingly and rapidly sketched the details of Gosslen's scheme to sweep Hackberry clean. There was a stunned silence when he finished as if the three men could not believe the depths of Gosslen's depravity.

"Ach!" said Gerbode finally, "neffer didt I like dott Gosslen budt dis iss doo much. Idt iss impossibles! Absoludely impossibles!"

"It kinda floors me, too," said Pres. "I allus pegged Gosslen for a buzzard gettin' fat off other folks' tough luck." He shook his head in wonderment at his own stupidity. "If Autry says that's the way she lays," went on Pres, "I'm with him from soda to hock. How 'bout you, 'Relio?"

Baca lighted a small, black *cigarrillo* and his face was expressionless in the match flame. "I have not bothered myself with Hackberry's affairs," he said gravely, "but it appears that the time has come when I should. Have you any legal authority to act in this matter, Mr. Autry?"

Gene nodded and produced his credentials.

Baca studied them quickly and returned them to Gene with a bow. "Burton Mossman is a friend of mine," he said, "ever since he first came to the territory." He turned his level gaze on Gerbode. "Herman, my friend," said Baca, "I assure you that I would be proud to carry such papers as does Mr. Autry."

"All righdt, all righdt," said Hermie, "I do voteffer iss pest."

Pres levered a shell into the breech of his rifle and eased the hammer down to half-cock. "I vote we try this case under the Winchester Act," he said. "They ain't many successful appeals to a higher court when you hand down the verdict."

Gene shook his head emphatically. "We must permit them to think their scheme has succeeded," he said.

Gerbode's face registered extreme dismay. "Vee musdt ledt dem der moneys steal?" he sputtered.

"It is the only way," said Gene patiently. "Suppose we catch Nolan with the money, we have caught only a minor member of the gang. If we grab Gosslen after he has been passed the money in Jordan's office, he will simply say that he was returning it to the rightful owners and that Jordan must have been an accomplice of the masked rider. Jordan says he doesn't know anything about it and that Gosslen is trying to frame him. We wind up with a twisty story all around and the odds are that Gosslen wiggles out of it. We can always trap Jordan on the rustled steers but that still leaves Gosslen in the clear and he is the man we have to catch red-handed. He is the leader of the Ladder gang and its brains."

"Mr. Autry is correct," said Aurelio Baca. "I for one am convinced that his is the only solution."

"I guess it is," said Pres as he regretfully fondled the stock of his rifle, "but I surelee hope that somebody gives me a little excuse to bust a cap in their direction. Hermie," said Pres, "don't you argue no more or I'll sit on you for your own good."

"All righdt," said Hermie reluctantly, "but if somedings gewrong happens py der moneys, I sharge you undt Raylio doubles in der store foreffer afters undt dondt vorgets it."

"It would be better," said Gene, "if we had time to secure the services of Mr. Baca's relatives. It would provide a margin of safety against possible slips but we don't have the time. One thing we must do, my presence during the entire robbery must be accounted for by men whose reputations will carry weight before the Territorial Court in Phoenix. Pres, you take your position in the stables where you can watch Champ every minute and thus swear on oath that he was not used by the masked rider supposedly me."

Pres nodded. "I'll get there right now," he said, and left the gathering. Cal jumped up to follow him but Gene waved him back.

"Hermie," said Gene, "after you empty the trash out the back door, be sure you don't lock it. Then bend over the case of currency until you get held up. I don't want Nolan to have any excuse to slug you. When he locks you in the bank, don't make a sound until you are sure he has crossed the street. You can see his dust out the window. Then raise the roof."

"Many tings haff I done already in mein life," said Gerbode, "budt neffer yet an ackdoor. I dry."

Gene gained a deeper respect for the rotund merchant in this moment. His was a dangerous assignment but never a word about it came from Hermie.

"Baca, you and Cal come up on the roof with me," said Gene. "I want you to watch the street and me at the same time. I want you to see Jordan give the signal, see the rider cross the street, see him throw the sack into Jordan's office, see Gosslen leave that office with his brief case, and be prepared to account for my whereabouts while all this is going on."

Baca nodded and Cal's eyes danced with excitement.

The noise of tables being laden with breakfast dishes came from the dining-room. Mrs. Gerbode's voice called loudly for Hermie, "Poppa!"

Hermie looked at his heavy silver watch. "Dime to opens up," he said, "better you look a liddle oudt and from der roof get." He waddled into the dining-room to open the front door.

Gene led the way up the vertical ladder steps that gave access to the roof through a square hatch covered with a heavy plank door. 'Relio and Cal followed hard on his heels and Gene motioned them to keep their heads below the level of the parapet while he pulled the hatch cover back into position. He had to leave an opening big enough to keep him posted on events below. If some quirk in Nolan's warped brain made him disregard Gosslen's instructions against murder, Gene had to protect Hermie.

Gene turned from the hatch cover when it was arranged to his satisfaction, to find 'Relio busy cleaning a bird nest out of the loophole he had selected to watch through. Cal was engaged in a similar task at the far corner of the roof. Gene felt a warm glow of comradeship at the way Baca had gone quickly about

*'Relio and Cal Followed Gene*

the business at hand. Gene crouched low and darted over to Baca for a final word.

"Can you see Jordan's office door, 'Relio?" he asked.

"Like in the front sight of a rifle," said Baca.

"No more than I expected of you," said Gene. "I feel proud to have you on my side."

"I am proud to be with you, Señor Autree," said 'Relio, purposely accenting Gene's last name in the Spanish fashion.

"You call me Gene, *por favor, Don Aurelio*," said Gene with a grin, "and we'll both feel better."

Baca smiled and stuck out his hand.

"When you see Gosslen give the signal, let me know," said Gene. "I have to keep an eye on Gerbode at the crucial moment."

"I will do better than that," said 'Relio. "The young *novio*, the boy with Pres, is down at the far corner where he can observe Gosslen's progress up the street. He will whistle so very softly to me when he espies the approach of that—that person. That will give you ample notice of what is coming and I myself will whistle when the signal is given from Gosslen to Nolan."

Gene was satisfied with these arrangements and stalked back to the hatch cover. The three allies waited tensely at their respective stations for the acts that would trap the Ladder gang.

It seemed to Gene that the wait was endless, but

in reality, they had only just gotten to their posts in time. A low whistle from Cal indicated Gosslen's approach up the street. A brief wait and 'Relio whistled sweet and low that Gosslen had stepped up to the door of Jordan's office and given Nolan the signal. Gene glued his eye to the slit in the hatch cover and shaded it with his hat so no trace of daylight could lance through from above and catch Nolan's eye in warning.

Gene's field of vision was limited to Hermie Gerbode where he knelt over the opened packing case filled with crisp, metal-strapped sheafs of new currency. Hermie was methodically lifting the bundles from the case and stacking them on the floor beside him when a masked figure stepped softly behind him and jammed a pistol muzzle in his back. The action was soundless and Gene had the funny feeling that he was watching a nickelodeon film.

Gerbode raised his hands above his head. The masked figure prodded him with the gun barrel and they moved out of sight toward the corner of the store that held the bank. A door swung open, a few indistinct words in a flat-toned voice floated up to Gene, the door clicked shut with the sound of a turning key, and Nolan walked stealthily back to the packing case. Gene breathed a sigh of relief. Gerbode was out of danger.

Nolan had an empty barley sack in one hand and his gun in the other. He slid the gun back into its holster and used both hands to cram the currency into the sack. Just before he finished looting the opened case marked DRY GOODS, Nolan hurriedly slipped two bundles of currency beneath his shirt.

Gene nodded to himself as if he had expected this very thing to happen. There was no honor among thieves and Nolan had trapped himself irrevocably through his own greed.

Nolan took a quick look around him, as if making sure that no one had seen him break faith with his partners in crime, and then stepped backward out of Gene's field of vision.

Gene levered his long body around and whispered sibilantly to 'Relio.

"Nolan's on his way," he said.

Baca nodded and glued his eye to his loophole. The sound of frantic hoofs drummed up out of the alley and a cloud of dust rose slowly above the level of the parapet wall.

'Relio tensed as he witnessed the culmination of Gosslen's plotting. A sorrel horse shot across the street with winking lights reflected from his saddle. Horse, rider, and saddle were enveloped in a haze of dust. As the racing horse came abreast of the sign saying *Town Marshal*, a fleeting object bridged the gap between horse and door. The dust cloud raced across the railroad tracks and was lost behind a screen of cottonwoods. 'Relio turned to Gene with a satisfied look on his face.

"Just as you said it would happen," he said. "If there was money in that sack when Nolan threw it, Gosslen is our meat. What do we do now?"

"We do the hardest thing in the world," said Gene. "We wait until it's safe to go down and have some breakfast."

"It is hard to wait," agreed Aurelio, "that I know for a surety. Also, I, too, am hungry. But is there nothing else for us to do but to sit and gaze upon the so beautiful morning?"

"You can keep an eye glued to that loophole," said Gene, "just to make sure you see Gosslen come out of Jordan's office when the sign is right."

'Relio nodded and again gave his attention to the loophole.

Gene whistled softly and Cal joined him by the hatch cover. The two of them stretched out on the roof while the morning sun slowly warmed their backs.

A terrific clamor suddenly welled up inside the store below them. Frantic door rattlings were accompanied by muffled cries, full of sound and fury. The noise increased to a crescendo of desperation and the door from the dining-room into the store burst open as Jordan played his part in the scheme of J. Francis Gosslen.

"Whut's goin' on in here?" roared his heavy voice. Then in feigned recognition of the location whence came the sounds, he began to run toward the bank door. The sound of the door being shaken on its hinges was deafening. Then Jordan bellowed a warning, "Stan' back while I shoots thuh lock off!" The report was thunderous between the store walls and Hermie's voice floated up to Gene and Cal.

"Robbers undt bandits," he screamed. "All der moneys from der pank getaken. Quickly, Jordan, you shouldt somedings doo."

A little knot of people from the dining-room had been attracted by the uproar. They clustered close about Gerbode's gesticulating figure as he sputtered at Star Jordan.

"Whut money, Hermie?" asked Jordan in realistic bewilderment. "Whose was it and who took it?"

"All der moneys for der pank," wailed Hermie. "From dott gase he took dems. Look, only der pig bills iss gone. Do somedings, *dumkopf,* dundt standt der undt silly questions ask!" Hermie flailed his arms and erupted into a torrent of unintelligible German that had a low boiling point.

'Relio softly tapped Gene on the shoulder. "Gosslen just stepped out of Jordan's office," he said. "He had his brief case with him."

Gene nodded and signaled 'Relio to listen with them at the hatch cover.

Jordan seemed to have Hermie quieted down. "All right, Hermie," he yelled, "yuh been robbed! Who done it? Where'd he go to?"

Hermie seemed on the verge of exploding. "It voss

somevuns behindt me," he screamed. "Neffer didt
his vace I see. Vich vay didt he go? Such a stoopid!
On mein stomach I shouldt see vich vay yet?"

Jordan let out a bellow of baffled rage. "How do
I know whut tuh look fer if yuh didn't see him
yoreself?" he shouted in Hermie's face.

Hermie danced up and down and tugged at his
scanty fringe of hair.

A new voice entered the conversation, a composed
voice filled with conscious virtue. "I could not help
overhearing your remarks," said J. Francis Gosslen.
"Perhaps I can help you, Marshal."

"Whut is it?" rumbled Jordan. "I shore need
some help on this deal."

"Well," said Gosslen unctuously, "I had gone to
your office, Marshal, for you to sign some papers
when I heard a horse running past. It was so dusty, of
course, that I can't be sure, but the rider seemed to
be masked and the horse was a reddish color and he
seemed to be wearing a silver-mounted saddle."

"Say, thet reminds me," said Jordan quickly. "I
seen a sorrel horse with fancy riggin' a'standin' in
thuh alley when I come past fer breakfast. Never
give it no thought though."

A buzz of excited comment went up from the
group of spectators who still clustered about the
scene of the crime. "Who's ridin' a silver-mounted
rig?" said one. "An' a sorrel horse," piped in another.

Gosslen was quick to capitalize on these chance

remarks. "By the way, Marshal Jordan," he said, "wasn't that man who called himself Dean riding a silver-spangled outfit?"

"That's it for shore," cried Jordan with a ring of triumph. "He had a sorrel horse too. I thought thet dude looked suspicious. Whichaway'd he go?"

Gosslen seemed to think it over carefully. "Why, I didn't pay much attention to his direction, Marshal," he said. "I gave it no thought at the time. It seems to me that he crossed the tracks and headed down the valley. Maybe he went out to the Boxed H herd."

"I'll raise me a posse and get right after him," barked Jordan, glad to be out of the limelight.

"Do you need a posse, Marshal?" said Gosslen.

Jordan glared at him.

"After all," said Gosslen smoothly, "it will take time to raise a posse and the bandit will have that much more head start. Besides, Marshal," Gosslen's voice was acid, "there was only one robber, this man called Dean."

"I'll send some of muh Ladder riders tuh scout thuh Boxed H's," rumbled Jordan, "an' take after the bandit muhself." He strode from the store and a flurry of drumming hoofs indicated he had left the hitchrack in a hurry.

The crowd of spectators dispersed and Hermie and Gosslen were left alone by the looted case.

"A most unfortunate occurrence," purred Gosslen,

"I trust that you were insured against such a calamity?"

Hermie wrung his hands in seeming despair. "Nodt undtil der pank offishully geopens doss der inzurance abblye," he said. "It iss a dodal loss."

Gosslen made sympathetic noises behind his teeth. "A great pity," he said. "If I can be of service in any way, Mr. Gerbode, please let me know. I assure you that I want to see Hackberry have a bank to serve its needs."

"Yah, I ledt you know," said Hermie, on the verge of snatching the brief case from under Gosslen's arm. "Undt now, I vant to sidt down undt coundt der loss."

"Of course," said Gosslen, "I quite understand. Good day to you, sir."

Gosslen walked into the dining-room, closed the door behind him, passed leisurely toward the front of the building, stepped onto the porch, and turned down the street toward his house. The battered brief case was gripped under his left arm and the gold-headed cane swung jauntily in his right hand. Mr. Gosslen gave the distinct impression of a man well-pleased with the world as he found it.

Gene slid back the hatch cover on the roof as soon as he heard Gosslen shut the door into the dining-room. Hermie looked up at the three faces peering down.

"Go aheadt undt grin like shimpanzees," said

Hermie. "I am an ackdoor yet."

"You did a fine job," said Gene, trying to keep a straight face.

"Ja!" said Hermie explosively. "Vy dundt vee grabs Gosslen mit der boodle righdt here?"

"If we did that, Hermie," said Gene seriously, "we still don't have an airtight case and Jordan gets out of any implication in the robbery. Also, he might be able to lay the blame for rustling those steers on Nolan. Don't worry, Hermie."

"All righdt," said Hermie, "putt der moneys dundt komm back, I poots on anudder act you dundt laugh so much yet."

"Where's Pres?" said Cal anxiously, as soon as he hit the floor behind Gene and 'Relio. Hermie shrugged his shoulders and Cal ran out the back door to find his partner.

"Hermie," said 'Relio pleasantly, "as soon as your dining-room is empty, I crave to assimilate some breakfast. How about it?"

Hermie waddled over and opened the connecting door. He seemed dissatisfied by his brief inspection and his shoulders sagged resignedly. "Noddt only mein moneys I loose," he said, "but der gustomers doo. Komm aheadt you chokers, der dining-room iss empdty like der pank."

Cal burst in the back door as Gene and 'Relio were heading for the dining-room. His face was crumpled in a worried frown. "I couldn't find Pres out back," he said. "You don't think anything has happened to him, do you, Gene?"

Gene slid his arm around Cal's shoulder. "If anything's happened to Pres, it's a cinch that something a whole lot worse has happened to someone else," he said. "Don't you fret, Cal. Pres'll show up when you least expect it."

Pres didn't show up when they entered the diningroom, he was already there, seated at a back corner table. "It's closer to the kitchen," said Pres when the others joined him, "and you don't have to wait so long. Besides, it ain't easily seen from the front windows."

The little band of good men and true were enjoying Mother Gerbode's cooking when Micky Hardesty joined them. She looked as fresh and pretty as a desert wildflower after her short rest. While she, too, ate a hearty breakfast, Gene led the discussion of the morning's events until everyone present had a clear picture of how each movement had been dovetailed into the Gosslen plot Gene had sketched rapidly before the robbery.

"Are you all satisfied that this robbery was planned by Gosslen?" asked Gene finally. The looks on the faces around the table were all the answer he needed. "That's fine," said Gene grimly, "because this robbery and rustling are going to be handled legally and you want to be certain that you don't get crossed up when you testify at the trial."

"I can't see no profit in messin' around with trials and lawyers and juries," said Pres. "We can give 'em a short rope and a sharp drop ourselves. Saves time, trouble, and expense."

"Look at it this way, Pres," said Gene crisply. "You people over here have been clamoring for statehood for a long time now. If you go ahead and hang these jaspers out of hand, even if it is merited, some flag-flapping politician back East is going to scream himself hoarse that you're not ready for the responsibilities and privileges of self-government. Then you go on like you have in the past, getting a bunch of defeated *politicos* sent out here to govern you. Besides, you can't take the law in your own hands."

Pres seemed unconvinced but 'Relio nodded his head.

"I'd admire to hang the lot of them or stand them against a wall someplace," he said, "but Gene's way is the best."

"Vor my pardt," said Hermie, "I am more sadisfied yet ven der moneys iss py der pank safe again."

"Hermie," said Pres in mock disgust, "what mind you have is one track."

"Dott iss zo," said Hermie agreeably, "undt der are no svitches from der track neider."

Gene took a last swallow of coffee from his cup and got to his feet, hitching his holster into position with an instinctive gesture. "Guess it's about time for me to show up at Gosslen's and claim my pay for running off your horses, Miss Micky," he said.

The girl looked up at him with an eloquent appeal in her eyes for him to be careful.

Pres and 'Relio shoved back their chairs and stood up. "I allus did like to go to war on a full stomach," said Pres stretching luxuriously.

'Relio spoke to Hermie as he reached for his sombrero beneath his chair. "Hermie," he said, "sell me a shotgun and a box of double-aught shells. I might get a chance to prove the old saying that buckshot means burying!"

Gene appreciated the instant response of the two men but he couldn't permit them to accompany him. "This is where I go it alone," said Gene.

Pres's face dropped and 'Relio looked perplexed.

"It has to be that way," said Gene. "If the three of us start ambling down the street toward Gosslen's, all overweighted with artillery, he'll know something's up. He may ditch the money, even burn it, to keep from being caught with the goods. If I show up alone, he'll think that Jordan bungled the job again but he won't get leary because he thinks he has me where he wants me and there'll always be time to get rid of me. This is a one-man job, to catch him with the goods, and I'm the man."

"You been a one-man army right along," said Pres, "why don't you let some of the rest of us get in on the fun?"

"Why, Pres," said Gene gaily, "I intend to do just

that. You and 'Relio take your artillery and mosey down to the railroad pens to keep an eye on that Ladder herd until I get through with Gosslen. Those Boxed H steers will be wearing a Ladder brand by now and when Jordan sells them to that buyer, we'll have him dead to rights for rustling."

Pres and 'Relio nodded.

Micky wiped her mouth with her napkin and stood up, too. "I'll go with you," she said to Pres.

"You stay right here, Miss Micky," said Gene firmly, "where Hermie and his wife can keep an eye on you. We're going to turn the case card down at the railroad pens and I won't have you endangered if there's any fireworks."

Micky didn't pout, she wasn't the pouting kind, but her chin set stubbornly. There was a determined glint in her eyes that should have warned Gene not to expect passive acceptance of his orders.

"Come on, Calico Cat," said Pres. "I got to put you aboard the Limited 'fore it's too late."

Cal's disappointment was written across his face and Gene saw it.

He looked at Pres and let one eyelid droop significantly. "You better not waste time on that right now, Pres," said Gene. "There'll be other ways of getting Cal to California just as fast."

Pres accepted Gene's wink and his words without a question. Cal brightened visibly at this reprieve from sudden departure.

Gene led Champ out of the stables and swung lithely into the saddle just as the westbound Limited whistled as it cleared Dead Horse Canyon. The man and his horse headed down the street for the house of J. Francis Gosslen and a stunning surprise.

# CHAPTER ELEVEN

## THE LADDER TOPPLES

The whistle of the westbound Limited brought a smile to the face of J. Francis Gosslen as he knelt before the open safe in his living-room. Moving swiftly, but without haste, he carefully removed the contents of the safe and placed the papers on his desk. His fingers riffled through them with cool dexterity, like a gambler palming a deck of cards, as he sorted them into two piles.

He tied the smaller pile carefully with linen thread and tucked it in his brief case. His smile broadened wolfishly as he noted the crisp sheafs of yellow-backed currency that were already there. He placed the larger pile of papers in the unused fireplace and touched a match to them. The licking flames seemed to warm Gosslen's cold blood as he quickly scratched a few words on a piece of legal parchment and left the paper squarely in the center of his desk. With a backward glance to make sure that the papers in the fireplace were entirely consumed, Gosslen picked up his brief case in one hand and grasped his cane firmly in the other. He seemed almost merry as he closed the door of the house behind him for the last time.

226

Gene did not bother with the gate when he rode abreast of Gosslen's yard. Champ jumped the picket fence with ease and seemed to leap forward to the little porch. Gene vaulted from the saddle onto the porch without touching the ground and knocked on the door.

No sound of answering movement came from within the house. Gene knocked again. The house was silent and its very silence seemed reproachful, like an abandoned mine tunnel when the miner's hopes have fled. Some sixth sense stirred the short hairs on Gene's neck and he grasped the doorknob.

It twisted readily under his grip and the door swung inward on well-oiled hinges. Gene swept the room with a practiced eye. It was just as it had been the night before except for the open safe. Warning impulses rippled along Gene's nerves.

Little wisps of charred paper fluttered in the fireplace from the draft of the opened door. The paper Gosslen had left in the center of his desk slid toward its edge with dry whisperings. One, two, three quick strides brought Gene to the desk and he seized the paper in eager hands.

Its message was short and sweet and filled with contempt for the man Gosslen had used so adroitly. "My Dear Marshal," Gene read the words, "I trust that you will not regret the price you have paid for your Boxed H bargain." There was no signature. Jordan would know only too well who had written those disdainful words.

Gosslen had played his tools in crime for suckers and Gene realized that he, too, had underestimated Gosslen's capacity for double-dealing. The slow-spaced exhaust of the Limited's engine as it waited impatiently for the tender to be filled seemed to toll the death knell of Gene's hopes. The sound suddenly galvanized Gene into flashing action as the significance of Gosslen's scornful message to Jordan became crystal clear.

The Limited was scornful of Hackberry as befitted the crack train of a great railroad system. The vestibule doors remained tightly shut during the train's brief stop for water but this did not seem to worry J. Francis Gosslen. He walked calmly across the station platform to the nearest car, planted his briefcase firmly between his feet, and rapped imperiously on the vestibule door with his cane. The noise brought a porter hastening down the length of his car to answer the summons of a waiting passenger.

Champ's sliding stop was masked by the station building. Gene lit running but when he rounded the corner of the station, he was cat-footedly stalking the arch criminal. His quick eyes took in the situation at a glance and noted the white jacket of the porter flashing past the windows of his car. Gene was about to hurl himself across the intervening space when the window of the station that faced the platform slid up and the station agent yelled a message to Gosslen.

*Gene Was About to Hurl Himself at Gosslen*

Gene ducked behind the corner of the station as Gosslen turned his head.

"Just got a telegram for Jordan," yelled the agent. "When you see him, tell him his buyer won't be in 'till the night combination." The agent ducked his head inside and closed the window as the chattering key again clamored for his attention. Gosslen nodded in understanding of the message he had no intention of delivering and rapped again on the vestibule door.

Gene glided across the intervening space with the speed and quiet of a leaping puma. Gosslen rapped again on the door, his cane upraised in furious tattoo, when a voice spoke softly almost in his ear.

"I've come to collect, Gosslen," said Gene.

Gosslen wheeled and lunged in the same moment, a snarl curling the corners of his mouth. There was a click at the head of his cane as he turned and a deadly stiletto blade snapped clear of the cane point to lick across Gene's ribs like a fiery ribbon. The warm blood welled down Gene's side but he hardly knew he had been touched so great was his rage. His instinctive twist away from Gosslen's thrusting arm had put him in striking position and he crossed a jarring left hand to Gosslen's temple.

Gosslen staggered back, still gripping his cane, and clutched frantically for the precious brief case as the Limited began to move. A startled porter swung open the vestibule door, took one look at the expression on Gene's face and slammed the door shut again as the train gathered speed.

Gosslen's face wore the look of a trapped coyote. He made a desperate thrust with the deadly cane. Gene dodged the thrust and raised a powerful right uppercut that lifted Gosslen to his tiptoe height. Gosslen's face slowly went blank as he sagged limply to the cinders.

Gene grabbed Gosslen and the brief case in one motion, kicked the gold-headed cane under the wheels of the Limited, and dragged his quarry around the corner of the station just in time. Star Jordan pounded up to the other end of the station on a lathered horse and swung heavily to the ground.

Jordan's heavy stubbled face showed his murderous mood. Johnny Hines and Banning had stuck to him like a mustard plaster insisting that he find Miss Hardesty. Jordan had had the devil's own time shaking them loose and he snorted to himself as he thought about it. *Find the girl they said.* He'd find her all right just as soon as he and the buyer came to terms on the Ladder herd in the stockyards, a herd mysteriously larger since the previous night.

Jordan pounded down the station platform peering anxiously around him. The Limited was disappearing around the bend in the track beyond the station and there was no buyer standing on the platform. Jordan looked puzzled. He rapped angrily on the station window. It slid up slowly and Jordan's voice seemed to accuse the station agent of hiding the man he sought. "Where's thet buyer?" thundered Jordan.

The agent's voice was tinged with petty irritation. "I just got through telling Gosslen to give you the message," he snapped. "He was standing right out there before the Limited pulled out." His own last words seemed to affect the agent like a dose of bitter salts. His voice trembled and broke. "Gosslen must have climbed aboard her and he ain't paid me yet for helping you play that joke," he cried and his words were an anguished wail.

Jordan's slow mind took a little longer before he, too, felt the full impact behind the agent's stricken moan. He unloosed a torrent of loud profanity that rattled the station window. The agent hurriedly slammed it shut and crouched behind his desk, fearful that Jordan would vent his spite on the first person he saw handy.

Gene felt the warm blood trickling down his side and soaking into the waist-band of his trousers but he knew that no muscles had been cut. If his wound didn't bleed too freely for too long, he was all right and he had no time to spare right now. He busied himself with the just-conscious Gosslen, smiling grimly at the fate that had delivered Jordan into his hands at the psychological moment.

Gosslen's hands were tied behind his back with Gene's silk neckerchief. His own black string tie was knotted through the handle of the brief case and the brief case, itself, thumped heavily against his chest as Gene dragged him to his feet. "You'd better tell Jordan about the high price he almost paid for the Boxed H's," said Gene, and Gosslen quaked with fear. Gene propelled him around the corner of the station and sent him staggering toward Jordan with a final shove.

Jordan's bellow of rage turned to a roar of unholy delight. He lunged for the hapless Gosslen mouthing maledictions. One hamlike hand tried to tear the brief case loose by main force and the other hand closed around Gosslen's long neck and raised him off his feet.

The inexorable pressure against Gosslen's windpipe was enough to kill him without the frenzied jerks with which Jordan tried to snatch the brief case loose from its moorings. Gosslen's body whipped to and fro from Jordan's lunges like an aspen leaf in a high wind. His face was turning a sickly greenish-blue when Gene stepped out in the open, his hat held carelessly in his right hand, to face Jordan squarely.

"Don't kill him, Jordan!" barked Gene. "You've got plenty to answer for without that."

Jordan's powerful hands relaxed their grip on both throat and brief case. Gosslen dropped to the cinders whimpering pitifully in his throat and flopped around like a netted trout as he sucked air into his tortured lungs.

Gene seemingly let his eyes follow Gosslen's movements and Jordan whipped his hand toward his shoulder gun. Gene had anticipated this move on Jordan's part. His right hand flicked forward and his heavy hat scaled squarely into Jordan's face. Gene leaped forward behind it and as Jordan's hand snaked back from the holster, Gene hit his arm just above the wrist a terrific chopping stroke with the side of his hand. The short-barreled gun exploded in mid-air as it dropped from Jordan's nerveless fingers. Gene stepped back and drew his own gun in the same movement. "Turn around, you scum, and get your hands up!" he snapped.

A look of sickly fear contorted Jordan's repulsive face. "Yuh aint—yuh can't—yuh wouldn't shoot me in thuh back," he pleaded, trying to reach the sun with his fingertips.

"It's no more than you got coming," said Gene, "but I don't play it your way. Now shut up, you make me sick listening to you." Gene ran one hand over the marshal's body in practiced search for hidden weapons but found none. He jammed his gun muzzle into Jordan's backbone as a reminder not to try any funny stuff and reached his hand around to unfasten the bright badge of the law from Jordan's vest.

Gene threw the star as far as he could throw it. "The next man who stands for the law in Hackberry would hate himself, if he had to wear what your dirty soul has tarnished," he said coldly, and stepped back ten paces from the gross bulk before him. Jordan gave off the rancid odor of perspiration inspired by fear.

Gene eased his gun into its holster and noiselessly unbuckled his gun belt. "Turn around, Jordan!" he snapped and the huge figure turned slowly as if he expected to meet a blast of hot lead from Gene's gun. His little pig eyes opened in amazement as Gene tossed his gun and belt aside and faced him with his arms hanging at his sides.

"If you've the courage, Jordan," said Gene, "here's your chance to take a licking in a fair fight before they put you and your talkative partner there behind the same barred windows." He nodded toward the prostrate Gosslen, who was curled around the brief-case, partially recovered from Jordan's strangling. Gosslen's eyes glittered venomously.

Jordan snarled wolfishly and launched himself toward Gene with widespread arms. Jordan had never met a man who could match his own brute strength. He ached with desire to close his hands on this taunting stranger who had destroyed all his evil hopes.

Gene waited for the charge with his body perfectly poised on the balls of his feet. Jordan was almost on top of him when Gene stabbed him with a straight left and pivoted sharply.

The watching Gosslen saw his chance and took it in characteristic fashion. He uncurled one leg in as lashing a blow as he could manage. It was strong enough to make Gene stumble, then fall, as it caught him in mid-pivot. Gosslen screamed at Jordan. "I got him, Jordan, I helped you. Kill him and we split only two ways."

Jordan gave no sign that he had heard his erstwhile commander. He wheeled his huge frame to charge back upon Gene who was facing him on his knees. Jordan sprang through the air, his thumbs extended to gouge the eye-sockets and his knees drawn up to smash into Gene's groin. Gene rolled back onto his shoulders and caught Jordan's chest on his boots in the same motion. Gene straightened his legs with the force of twin pistons and Jordan hurtled through the air to hit the station wall with a stunning smash.

Gosslen, still groggy from the punishment he had absorbed, scrambled to his feet with only one insane desire—to run, run, run—anyplace, anywhere away from this avenging angel with the name of Gene Autry. He had forgotten, if he ever knew, that hands and arms make a big difference in balancing a running body. His were tied behind him, and in addition, his bulging brief case thumped and swayed against his chest. He made several frantic stumbling steps and fell. He got up and tried again with the same result. Gosslen gave up and lay still, twitching like a trapped rabbit.

Gene was on his feet instantly after Jordan's unwitting tumbling act and a quick glance at Gosslen told him the whole story. He turned his full attention to finishing off Jordan.

The beefy ex-marshal was on his feet when Gene hit him; an open hand slap with a stiff arm that left a dull red glow behind it. Jordan seemed to snap back to consciousness with the impact and grunted profanely. Gene rocked him with short arm jolts to the belly and Jordan cursed with each blow. He clubbed Gene about the head and shoulders with his thick forearms as Gene consistently kept inside his reach. A straight left with Gene's whole body behind it snapped Jordan's head like a puppet's. He lashed out with a booted leg as Gene stepped back. Gene dodged inside the wicked kick and brought Jordan's last chance to fight a fair battle to a crashing climax.

His right hand shot up under Jordan's kicking leg and forced it on upward. Jordan thudded to the platform and Gene pounced on his thrashing feet as though they were the horns of a steer. Grasping one booted foot by heel and toe, Gene twisted as if bull-dogging against time. Jordan flopped over on his face. Gene straddled his body, drawing the leg forward and increasing his pressure. Jordan bawled for mercy.

Gene suddenly released his grip and before Jordan could make a move, Gene grasped his flannel shirt on both sides just above the belt and lunged forward. The shirt peeled up above Jordan's head, pinioning both arms as securely as though they were strait-jacketed. Gene swiftly tied the shirttails together, cinching them down with the knot, until Jordan was worse than helpless. The more Jordan strove to lower his arms and unpeel the shirt, the tighter the knot became. His slow brain finally grasped the futility of struggle and he lay still, with a muffled stream of useless profanity welling up inside his shirt-swathed head.

Gene retrieved his gun and buckled it on while he took stock of personal damages. The slash from Gosslen's sword cane was a clean flesh wound, more painful than dangerous. He staunched the flow of blood with a clean cloth from his saddle bags. Champ snorted at the blood smell and nuzzled Gene affectionately when he was reassured that it was nothing to worry about.

Gene prodded the prostrate Jordan to his feet with his gun just to let him know that the fair fight was over and the day of reckoning had begun. Gosslen lay where he had collapsed the last time. Gene told him to get up and Gosslen sullenly shook his head. Gene swung into his saddle and shook out a loop in his riata.

"You can walk, Gosslen," he said, "or I can drag you. Make it easy on yourself."

Gosslen read the determination in Gene's voice and scrambled to his feet. "Now walk over there in front of Jordan," said Gene curtly, and Gosslen did what he was told.

When the two crooks were in position, Gosslen in

front and Jordan close behind him, Gene spread his loop over them both and drew it tight without unneccessary roughness. "You know the way to Gerbode's Store, Gosslen," said Gene. "Start walking!" The brief case knocked against Gosslen's chest like the drum beat of doom as he led the little procession up the main street of Hackberry for all to see. He was leading Jordan again but not in the way he had planned it so carefully.

They were no more than half-way from the station to the store when Micky Hardesty walked briskly down the street toward them. Gene saw her and called her name but she would not look at him. Her determined chin was set and she walked past them with a free, swinging stride and headed toward the railroad pens. She had Gene where he couldn't stop her and she knew it.

So did Gene. He had to deliver his prisoners to a safe haven. He smiled in admiration at Micky's spunk but knew she might prove to be an embarrassing hindrance if Nolan showed fight. Gene urged his little caravan into a faster gait.

The news of their coming had preceded them. Hermie was standing on the porch when Gene and Champ halted before the store. Hermie's eyes fastened on the brief case and he made excited motions with his hands.

Gene cut the brief case loose and handed it over to Gerbode. "You better count it, Hermie," said Gene,

"Gosslen might have robbed himself. We'll get the rest of it when we get Nolan."

"Gounting idt will a pleasures be," said Hermie, grasping the precious object. "Budt virst, vott about doze—doze beeples you gott lazzoed?"

"I was going to ask you if you had a safe place to keep them," said Gene.

"You pet my life," said Hermie joyfully. "In der pank I geeps dem, mitt a shodtguns in mein own handts undt a leedle brayer dey drys somedings."

"Get the shotgun," said Gene, "and they're all yours."

Hermie almost knocked his hat off getting into the store. Gene carefully removed his loop from the two dejected men. All the fight had gone out of Jordan still inside his smothering shirt that enveloped him like a hangman's hood. Gosslen was filled with an abject terror that was self-inspired. He knew what he would have done with his prisoners if the position had been reversed and the knowledge tortured him with apprehensions of his own fate. He seemed almost relieved when Hermie stepped out of the store again with the biggest shotgun he could find in stock.

"Achtung!" barked Hermie at the two men in the street. "Vorwarts marsh!" Gosslen plodded up the steps to the porch, not bothering to lend Jordan a hand as he stumbled behind him. Hermie shepherded them both inside and Gene wheeled Champ for the stockyards as he heard Hermie's instructions.

"Chust sidt inzide der pank," said Hermie, "undt gontemplates. I sidt py der door oudtzide yet mitt der scatter guns."

Gene eased Champ around the corner of the stock-yards in time to hear Micky's angry voice.

"My steers are in there," she said, "I know they are."

Micky teetered precariously on the stockyard fence, outraged anger in every line of her lithe young body. Pres and Cal sat between her and the gate while Aurelio sat watchfully on the opposite side of the gate. Pres and 'Relio had hooked their boot heels inside the plank below them for balance, thus leaving both hands free to handle the long guns they held across their laps.

Nolan sat a dusty sorrel horse out from the gate, level with Micky on the fence. He knew something was wrong with the plans and his cold eyes flickered warily from Micky and the fence-sitters to Johnny and Banning who sat their horses squarely in front of the gate.

"Those are my steers in there with the others," repeated Micky angrily, "you turn them out." She spoke straight at Nolan.

"Cain't do it," said Nolan flatly. "Done sent all muh riders out lookin' fer thet bank robber."

"That's no excuse," snapped Micky. "There are riders right here." She pointed to Johnny and to

Banning who glared at Nolan.

"Them cattle belong tuh Star Jordan," said Nolan. "They're wearin' his brand, all of 'em. I don't aim to turn 'em out lessen he orders me tuh. Thet's final."

Gene inwardly berated Johnny for not taking a position between Nolan and the girl. Everybody was bunched either to one side or in front of the gunman. Gene gathered himself for instant action and alerted Champ with a signaling knee.

"You better ride up to the bank, Nolan," said Gene crisply. "Jordan's up there—and Gosslen, too. You can get your last orders from them. And Nolan, you can return those bundles of bills you stuffed under your shirt awhile back."

Nolan knew how completely wrong all the Ladder gang plans had gone. He drove his right spur home with cruel force. The tired sorrel snorted and jumped sideways against the fence.

Gene launched Champ across the hard-packed ground with a wild rebel yell on his lips.

Nolan swept Micky off the fence and across his saddle for a hostage while his six-gun cleared its holster a split second too late. He thumbed back the hammer and Gene thrust his own hand forward between the hammer of Nolan's gun and the cartridge chamber.

Nolan squeezed the trigger in frantic haste and the heavy hammer pin bit deep into Gene's hand between thumb and forefinger. Despite the biting pain, Gene closed his hand around the cylinder and trigger guard. He wrenched the gun from Nolan's grasp with a mighty wrenching surge of power that brought his hand up level with Nolan's neck. Gene's arm snapped out and around Nolan's neck like a steel trap and his whipcord muscles braced themselves against the shock as Champ's plunging momentum dragged Nolan strangling from his saddle.

Micky slid off the saddle onto the ground and Johnny Hines seemed to lose his dazed expression as he sprang from his saddle and ran toward her.

Gene wheeled Champ with Nolan thrashing wildly in the crook of his arm to see Johnny lift Micky's tousled head tenderly in his arms. Gene straightened his own arm and Nolan sagged to the ground. Pres, Cal, and 'Relio still sat on the fence in gaping amazement at the speed with which Gene had acted. Gene looked at Banning and raised his voice.

"Rock on over here, Boomer," he called. "You look like the only one in his right mind."

Banning trotted over with an ear-splitting grin on his grizzled face. "Yu' give th' orders, boss," he said.

Gene pointed at Nolan. "Dab your loop on that hunk of coyote bait," he said, "and herd him up to Gerbode's to join his partners. You can help Hermie guard them if he'll let you."

"It's goin' tuh be a pleasure," said Banning. "It'd be a lot more pleasant if yu'd give me his gun. I'd

admire tuh use it on him after him a'tryin' to man-
handle Miss Micky just now." He dropped his grass
rope around Nolan's neck as he talked.

Gene carefully withdrew the hammer from its
biting hold in the web of his hand. The wound was
painful but not serious and it bled freely before he
bound it up, which was a good sign.

Banning took the gun with obvious relish. "Hup-
pah," he yelled at Nolan, jerking him to his feet.
"Drag yore dew-claws. Yore shore th' sorriest critter
I ever had in my loop."

"Micky, Micky, Micky," crooned Johnny, as
though soothing an unbroken colt. The girl slowly
opened her eyes behind fluttering lashes.

"Where's Gene?" she asked murmuring his name.

Johnny was unabashed. "He's doin' what he does
best," he said. "An' so am I." He tightened his arms.

Micky sprang to her feet with remarkable recovery
of health. "You'll have to prove that to me when I'm
not weak from shock," she said, and climbed back
on the fence.

*I hope the conductor on that freight sent the mes-
sage I gave him last night,* thought Gene to himself.
*This is no place for me—man might get hurt or
married.* He rode over to the fence and climbed up
with the others.

One by one, Gene pointed out the five steers that
he and Johnny had worked over the night before.
Each one wore the Ladder brand.

"They must have re-branded through a wet blanket," said Gene. "There isn't a raw scar on a single one of Miss Hardesty's steers."

"It will show up when we skin them, though," said Aurelio.

"You don't have to kill them," said Gene. "Each of those five steers is packing a silver dollar in a slit in his dewlap and the slit is pinned together with a horseshoe nail. We were in such a hurry last night that Johnny used the five he had bet with Jordan on that bronc ride. All the money he had but he swore it was in a good cause."

Johnny twisted sheepishly on the fence at Gene's kidding.

"Who done the thinkin' and chipped in the nails?" asked Pres quietly.

"Gene," yelped Johnny excitedly, and his voice showed the pride he felt in his friend.

Micky looked from one to the other of the two men who had saved her steers and herself. Gene was an eye-filling sight and he had the brains and the brawn to back it up. Johnny appealed to the eternal feminine instinct in her. Micky almost shook hands with herself. Not many girls had a chance to choose between two men like Gene and Johnny.

Gene saw the look in Micky's eye and grinned inwardly. He had spotted a plume of smoke racing toward Hackberry from the west and his keen sight had seen the skeleton train behind it. His stay in

Hackberry was nearly over.

"Are you gentlemen satisfied with the evidence?" he asked Pres and 'Relio.

They nodded.

"With me and 'Relio and Hermie and you to swear to the robbery and Mis' Hardesty and Hines and Banning to swear to the rustlin' along with us," said Pres, "we surelee got enough to make the governor sit up and take notice."

"Don't forget Cal," said Gene seriously. "He's the best witness of all. He's the only one who didn't savvy the country and the people well enough to imagine what's happened. You savvy it now, though, don't you, Cal?"

Cal nodded vigorously. "And I know another thing, too," he said.

"What's that?" asked Pres quickly.

"You can't tell a man or a horse by what they wear," said Cal and grinned at Pres Wesley.

"We better get over to the station," said Gene with a quick glance at the west. "I want to send a couple of telegrams. One to Mossman telling him I don't need his commission as Special Ranger any longer, and one to the governor telling him what's happened and asking him to make Pres or 'Relio Deputy Territorial Marshal for Hackberry."

"Make it 'Relio," said Pres. "I'll feel better. If I get to enjoyin' town life too much, 'Relio can persuade me into the *jusgado* and Hermie can lend me

*"Are You All Satisfied With the Evidence?"*

enough to pay my fine. Besides which, 'Relio can always raise him a posse just by deputizing his relatives. Me, I'm a jerk-line freighter and I don't crave to be nothin' else."

"I ask for nothing better than always to have you call me friend," said 'Relio to Pres. Then he turned to Gene.

"What about those men riding for the Ladder outfit?" he asked.

"I don't think they'll give you any trouble," said Gene. "The brains of the gang and the deadly killers are trapped. The rest of 'em were just taking the easy way to make a dollar. They'll come riding in from their fake search, find the jig is up and I think they'll be real glad to turn state's evidence and save their own skins."

'Relio nodded and the little group filed into the station.

The station agent breathed a sigh of relief when he saw that his name was not included in the telegrams he sent for Gene. The sound of his key died away as he signed off Gene's message to the governor and the agent suddenly stiffened. A drumming forefinger was sending him a message, tapping out the code on the office counter. Gene signed off and the agent's pencil drummed his swift reply — I'VE LEARNED MY LESSON. Gene nodded and the agent lowered his head with a thankful heart.

They were all standing on the station platform,

linked in the bonds that had been established by their association with Gene in breaking up the Golden Ladder, when a bob-tail train backed off the turning wye and eased to a stop at Hackberry station, headed west. A high-wheeled Pacific type engine was coupled to a long steel car that looked half-express and half-passenger. A sliding door in the center of the car opened and a trainman pushed a cleated gangway onto the platform.

The trainman picked Gene out of the crowd immediately. He walked down the gangway and stepped up to him, "You must be Autry," he said.

Gene nodded.

"The railroad wouldn't have highballed this car out on blind orders for nobody else," he said admiringly. "They told me to take orders from you. We leave when you say so, and they'll give us a high-iron all the way."

"I'm ready now," said Gene. "Come on, Cal, you'll arrive in California in style. We'll have to come back as witnesses, and you'll see all these folks again."

Cal said a hasty good-by to everyone at once, with a special handshake for Pres, and bounded up the gangway almost on Champ's heels. He had a question or six ready and waiting when Gene pulled in the gangway behind him and dropped the safety bar across the door.

Gene and Cal stood in the open door of the special car, Champ's stall and manger at one end, bunks, table and cookstove at the other, for a last look at the station platform. The engineer eased the throttle forward and the high drivers began to hum the song of the rails.

Johnny Hines slipped his arm around Micky's waist and waved a final salute with his free hand. Micky pretended to slap him but it was only a gesture.

"Gene," began Cal, and stopped at the look on Gene's face. "What's the matter, Gene?" he asked anxiously.

"You look out there on the platform, Cal," said Gene in mock worry. "Johnny Hines has tied onto something he'll have to handle without my help."

# WHITMAN BOOKS
# FOR BOYS AND GIRLS

## NEW STORIES
## OF ADVENTURE AND MYSTERY

The books listed above may be purchased at
the same store where you secured this book.

# WHITMAN BOOKS
# FOR BOYS AND GIRLS

## NEW STORIES
## OF ADVENTURE AND MYSTERY

Up-to-the-minute novels for boys and girls about favorite characters, all popular and well known—

ROY ROGERS and the Outlaws of Sundown Valley
ROY ROGERS and the Ghost of Mystery Rancho
ROY ROGERS and the Gopher Creek Gunman
ROY ROGERS and the Raiders of Sawtooth Ridge

GENE AUTRY and the Golden Ladder Gang
GENE AUTRY and the Thief River Outlaws
GENE AUTRY and the Redwood Pirates

ZANE GREY'S The Spirit of the Border
ZANE GREY'S The Last Trail

RED RYDER and the Adventure at Chimney Rock
RED RYDER and the Secret of the Lucky Mine

BLONDIE and DAGWOOD'S Adventure in Magic
BLONDIE and DAGWOOD'S Marvelous Invention